I0727296

THE HOUSEWIFE ASSASSIN'S GARDEN OF DEADLY DELIGHTS

JOSIE BROWN

A BOOK BY

SIGNAL
PRESS

"This is a super sexy and fun read that you shouldn't miss! A kick ass woman that can literally kick ass as well as cook and clean. Donna gives a whole new meaning to "taking out the trash."
—Mary Jacobs, *Book Hounds Reviews*

"*The Housewife Assassin's Handbook* by Josie Brown is a fun, sexy and intriguing mystery. Donna Stone is a great heroine —housewives can lead all sorts of double lives, but as an assassin? Who would have seen that one coming? It's a fast-paced read, the gadgets are awesome, and I could just picture Donna fighting off Russian gangsters and skinheads all the while having a pie at home cooling on the windowsill. As a housewife myself, this book was a fantastic escape that had me dreaming "if only" the whole way through. The book doesn't take itself too seriously, which makes for the perfect combination of mystery and humour."
—*Curled Up with a Good Book and a Cup of Tea*

"*The Housewife Assassin's Handbook* is a hilarious, laugh-out-loud read. Donna is a fantastic character–practical, witty, and kick-ass tough. There's plenty of action–both in and out of the bedroom… I especially love the housekeeping tips at the start of each chapter–each with its own deadly twist! This book is perfect for relaxing in the bath with after a long day. I can't wait to read the next in the series. Highly Recommended!"

"This was an addictive read–gritty but funny at the same time. I ended up reading it in just one evening and couldn't go to sleep until I knew what the outcome would be! It was action-packed and humorous from the start, and that continued throughout, I was pleased to discover that this is the first of a series and look forward to getting my hands on Book Two so I can see where life takes Donna and her family next!"

"The two halves of Donna's life make sense. As you follow her story, there's no point where you think of her as "Assassin Donna" vs. "Mummy Donna', her attitude to life is even throughout. I really like how well this is done. And as for Jack. I'll have one of those, please?"

And How Does YOUR Garden Grow?

Fresh cut, manicured lawns. A rainbow's hue of blooms. From the lushest tree to the thickest bush, every inch of a housewife's garden is scrutinized by her neighbors.

To ensure that others stare at it in awe (as opposed to glare at it in horror), follow these helpful hints:

- *Hint #1: Nurture your plants. Know their growth patterns, and their need for sun, water, and soil type — in the same way you know the life story, habits, and predilections of your targets. It's the only way to ensure you control their fates.*
- *Hint #2: Variety is the spice of life — and death. While succulent plums and crisp apples are fruits of your labor that you can actually eat, castor bean and rosary pea aren't really vegetables, but deadly poisons — good*

to know, in case there are a few accidents you can't wait to have happen. Angel's Trumpet tea, anyone?

- *Hint #3: Always add to your garden. A well-placed flowerbed does a lot to cover your yard's sins—and yours too, especially if you've got a corpse or two still lying around.*

A TINY, PORCELAIN BUDDHA—BARREL-BELLIED AND SQUINT-eyed from his clownishly wide grin—taunts me from the next table. I am sitting in the open street-side patio in the Happy Sun Dim Sum Emporium, on Grant Street in San Francisco's Chinatown, tailing my target on the last leg of his indiscriminate shopping spree. His name is Yang Cheng. He is an asset for the MSS—the People's Republic of China's Ministry of State Security—its covert-ops agency.

He has lousy taste in gifts.

Not only did he purchase the Buddha, but a vinyl Hello Kitty pencil box, and a Patek Philippe men's watch knock-off. All of these tchotchkes are actually made in his country before being shipped here, where they are purchased by tourists who don't realize that practically everything they already own is made in Chinese factories.

Yang eats alone, slurping down one *siu mai, bao, shu mai* and *har gow* after another. The dim sum carts, tinkling from the tins filled with their savory delights, don't get very far down the slim aisle by his sidewalk table before he stops them to peruse his next dish. From what I've counted, he has already chowed down on twenty of the aromatic pot stickers, as well as three pork steamed buns. If he keeps this up, he'll soon resemble his laughing Buddha.

Sometime during lunch, he'll be joined by someone. You see, his real purpose for being stateside has nothing to do with sightseeing and everything to do with stealing intel, which will be handed off to him sometime during his meal, and that he will take back with him to Beijing.

The majority of the restaurant's patrons are locals—mostly Chinese-American, but there is a smattering of Caucasian locals and tourists too. My mission partner, Jack, and I can easily be mistaken for the latter as we sit side-by-side, cuddling and cooing and making goo-goo eyes, like any couple on a weekend romp in America's most romantic city.

And, like everyone else, we use our cell phones to take photos of the food and selfies of ourselves enjoying it.

It may seem we're photographing each other, but in truth, we're documenting Yang's movements for our employer, the CIA-sanctioned black-ops organization, Acme Industries, for anything that may tip us off as to when the hand-off takes place.

Once it does, we'll make sure that Yang won't even get as far as the exotic green tile-roofed Dragon Gate at Chinatown's entrance before he is overcome with a fatal heart attack. It won't be the Chinese food that kills him, but a prick with a needle filled with aconite.

We don't know who is doing the drop, but we have satellite surveillance on the restaurant, so that our tech-op, Arnie

Locklear, can follow Yang's cutout to a final destination. He also sees what we see, through our special surveillance contacts.

"Incoming," Jack murmurs, as he takes a dumpling and holds it to my lips so that I can take a bite.

Even as I lick my lips and open wide, I shift my gaze toward Yang. Jack is right in one regard: Yang has been accosted by a little old lady. Her hair is gray, her skin is pocked, and her back is bowed with age. She stands outside the thin railing that separates the Happy Sun's tables from the rest of the sidewalk. Apparently, she is trying to sell him historic postcards of Chinatown. He waves her away while shouting back at her in Mandarin, but she is insistent. When she jabs a gnarled finger at one card in particular, something he sees there makes him stop mid-expletive. He grabs them out of one of her hands and shoves a ten-dollar bill into the other. She stuffs the bill deep into the folds of her shawl.

The Buddha is pocketed too.

"She's the cutout," I mutter.

"If that's the case, go after her," Jack insists. "There must have been something in the Buddha, and it's being passed off to someone else. Find out whom, while I take care of Yang."

As part of my cover, I give him a long, deep kiss. It's also part of my philosophy on life: live every moment as if it is your last.

As our lips part, I slip him the needle with the aconite and whisper, "Take the cards. By his reaction, they're obviously important."

He nods as he strokes my cheek. "Be careful," he mutters.

As I saunter out of the restaurant, I feel Yang's eyes upon me. I don't like the leer on his lips.

That's okay. It won't be there for long.

THE LITTLE OLD LADY WEAVES IN AND OUT OF THE THICK throng of tourists who are perusing the myriad of wares on the outside tables of the district's vendors.

She stops four blocks from the Happy Sun, beside a trio of old men who are playing authentic Chinese instruments, as if enthralled by their simple tune.

A young Asian man in black jeans and a leather jacket nudges her. They don't make eye contact, but he proves he has the Buddha when he tosses it in the air before pocketing it.

When she looks back, I turn toward a shop window displaying silk kimonos. Her reflection is clear enough for me to see the satisfied smirk on her face.

Then, suddenly, the smirk is gone, along with the rest of her face. Really, it was a mask. Now I see a beautiful Asian woman who looks to be in her late twenties. She also strips off the gloves—thin skin-like latex—that gave her hands an aged effect, and tosses all three items into a trashcan.

"Did you get a clean enough shot for a scan?" I ask Arnie.

"Clean enough," he assures me. Good. Hopefully, Acme's Facial Recognition software will reveal her true identity.

When I turn back around, she is climbing on a bus headed up Sacramento Street's steep incline.

On the other hand, her courier strides quickly down the street.

Quickly, I grab the gloves and mask from the trash. Then I run toward the courier, only to be blocked by a clerk insisting to a German tourist that the Bose speaker system in his hand can be purchased much more cheaply here than in Berlin.

By the time I get around the hagglers, it's too late. The courier has disappeared into thin air—

Or not. I pass a narrow alley wedged between a souvenir shop and a restaurant, the Crescent Moon. I hear footsteps. A slim shaft of light reveals the man. He pulls a brick from the wall and pulls out a key.

He gets the feeling that he's not alone. Slowly, he turns around. Seeing me, he frowns—

Then hurls the brick at me.

I duck just in time. The brick whizzes above my head by barely an inch.

By the time I've drawn my Sig Sauer P226R, he has already hopped onto one of the two motorcycles used by the Crescent Moon's delivery team—both Ducati Hypermotards —and is roaring down the alley.

Sure, I'm up for a ride.

The second bike's ignition key is tucked in the hole in the wall as well. I hop on, rev it up, and head down the alley until it dead-ends into another. But I've reached it just in time to see my target's bike climbing a stone stairwell.

When the courier reaches the top, he skids to a stop.

Damn it, my bullet just misses his ear. He's now duly warned that I mean business, and screeches off again.

Oh well, in for a dime, in for a dollar, right?

I open up the throttle on my bike so that it climbs the stairs too.

When my bike reaches the top, it clatters over the roof's clay tiles before landing onto the flat center beam. I brake hard to halt it from flying off into oblivion and crash-landing onto the unsuspecting tourists three stories below.

The courier is already on the far side of the roof. He zips over a long, narrow plank that connects a neighboring building's even steeper roof over an alleyway.

He makes the leap. As he roars off again, he turns back to wave at me, a wide grin on his face. Of course, he doesn't expect me to follow.

Wrong. My son's dirt biking scout badge came at the expense of many cuts and bruises—his and mine. Granted, as his troop's leader, I wasn't eligible for a badge. That's okay. The true reward of any skill is how you use it to your own advantage. I use it now, as I zoom off after the courier. I twist the throttle—

And over the alley I go.

As my motorcycle hits the slanted roof, it almost slips out from under me, but not quite. I rev the engine to keep my momentum. A second later, I crest the roof, skidding onto the center joist.

The courier's bike clatters on the clay tiles as it heads

toward the far side of the roof. I shoot for his head, but he ducks just in time.

He now realizes that his only chance to lose me is to leap onto another roof. Unfortunately for him, the closest building is at least a fifteen-foot jump. To make matters worse, its roof's pitch is even steeper than the last.

Heck, I wouldn't try it myself. But he's got no choice. Once again, he takes off—

And so does Buddha. It slips out of his pocket and clatters as it rolls down the roof's tiles, toward the street.

Realizing this, the courier brakes. He whips around.

This time, my bullet pierces him right between the eyes.

His head jerks back, but he's still holding on tight as his bike flies off the roof. The engine's roar can be heard echoing off the old walls of the alley below.

I spring from my Ducati and lunge for the Buddha. I grasp the figurine just as it falls off the roof—

But my balance is no better than Buddha's. I need one hand to hold him. The other holds tight to the building's gutter.

I'm dangling four stories over Grant Street, but at least I'm still alive—

For the moment, anyway. One by one, the rusty hinges that hold the copper gutter against the ancient Victorian groan as they give way.

I have only a few seconds to assess my situation. On the floor below me, a line of wash—several pairs of granny panties, diapers, and a sheet or two—is strung from one window to another. Two floors below it, an awning hangs over the entry of a street-level shop. It must be a bakery because the people streaming in and out are munching on sweet buns, petit fours, and almond cookies.

Ah, good times.

"Let go," Jack murmurs in my ear bud. Sometimes I resent the omnipotence of Acme's surveillance capabilities. I've got to admit, I appreciate it this very second.

"Only if you catch me," I grumble. *As if.*

"Let's give it a shot."

"Are you crazy? You can't see me through the awning! At the same time, I'll need the awning to break my fall!"

"I've got Arnie's eyes on you too, remember?"

"This will be fun!" Arnie pipes up. "We'll be like firemen catching a baby falling from a burning building."

Somewhere up in the heavens Arnie watches as I shake my head adamantly. "This isn't a game! It's my life!"

"Don't you trust me?" Jack teases me with his low chuckle.

Another hinge springs from the wall and drops onto the awning.

"Jump at the count of three," Jack suggests.

The gutter squeals as it swings away from the ledge. "Yeah, okay," I agree reluctantly.

"One," Jack says, "two—"

Too late.

I scream, "Three!" as I plummet four stories, tearing down the wash line as I go.

"A little to your left, Jack," Arnie says. "No…no I meant *my* left! Um—your right!"

Talk about the blind leading the blind.

The awning sags when I hit it, but thank goodness it's Sunbrella and I'm flung back into the air.

"Change of course! Change of course!" Arnie yells in my ear.

"I think I'll wing this," Jack assures him, if not me.

This time when I drop, I tear through the awning, but I'm able to seize a large swath of it and cling to it.

Jack holds tight too, as I land in his arms.

He cradles me until I'm ready to be set down.

There is a crowd around us. At first they stare, but soon they're cheering.

Especially when he kisses me. "Donna Stone, will you marry me?"

"Really?" I pout. "Jack Craig, which one of your five brain cells told you this is the time or the place?"

"Romantic San Francisco, a cheering crowd—" He sighs when he sees my frown. "Okay, you're right. I want a do-over."

"Just one," I warn him. "So make it count."

Noting the Buddha in my hand, one of the women working the bakery counter exclaims in Mandarin, "You see? Buddha brings good luck!"

I hope she's right. But something tells me that what he holds portends doom and gloom.

That doesn't mean I'll pass on the cookie she hands me.

Call it comfort food. Besides, I've worked off a few calories. I deserve it.

2

Family

The term "family" is the classification for plants that consist of similar genera. In most cases, plant families have similar needs for light, soil, and water. Shovels, hoes, and rakes are the tools that allow you to keep them healthy. Sprinkle liberally with organic fertilizer.

For humans, the term "family" is much the same—our siblings and we spring from the fertile loins of our mother and father, who in turn sprang from the fertile loins of their parents.

Human families have similar likenesses and dispositions. However, they are usually prone to petty squabbles, sibling rivalries and long-term jealousies, all the more reason to keep the hoes, rakes, and shovels out of reach when tempers flare.

Instead, nurture your family with kind words, and wonderful treats—none of which should be sprinkled with fertilizer, organic or other.

I KNOCK QUICKLY BEFORE OPENING JEFF'S BEDROOM DOOR. "You've been on your computer for two hours straight," I warn my twelve-year-old son. "Are you still working on homework?"

Before I can look at his computer, Jeff slams it shut.

Hmmm.

When a child looks guilty, a mother's mind is like a Quantum supercomputer, calculating all the possible variables as to why. Has he done, or said, anything that will bring shame on him or his family? If not, then what can she do, or say, to stop him before it's too late?

To his credit, Jeff doesn't have a devious bone in his body. Nor has he given me any reason to acquisition a full Interpol surveillance operation on him (whereas his older sister, Mary, has come close several times).

But a couple of months ago, he had the misfortune of walking into a terrorist situation at the hotel in which his school was holding its prom. Not only was he taken hostage, he was almost beheaded.

All the more reason to cut him some slack. Nothing changes a person's perspective quicker than a close call with death.

So that he'll presume I'm off the scent, I walk over to his bed on the pretense of straightening his comforter. Ever watchful, he swivels his desk chair. He attempts a faint smile, but it cannot mask the sadness in his eyes. As I ease down onto his bed, I ask, "What are you working on?"

"Finishing a project. Current Events." He shrugs. "Mr. Karman says it counts as half our grade, and it's due tomorrow."

I prop a pillow behind my back. "What did you choose as your topic?"

Jeff purses his lips. "Terrorism." He winces as he waits for my reaction.

I nod nonchalantly. "Timely topic."

He seems relieved that it hasn't upset me.

Actually, it has, but he doesn't need to know this. To cover this up, I force a smile on my face. "How is your paper coming?"

"There's so much information on it that it's practically writing itself." He opens his laptop. When the screen comes up, he beckons me forward. I stand over him as he pulls up several PowerPoint pages. "Look here! When mapping terrorism over the past fifty years, we see growth in the number of attacks, which now top out at over seven thousand per year around the world"—he points to a bar graph that calls out each year from 1974 to now—"whereas each year is substantially greater. Then the last three columns spike almost sky high. Also, the predominance of acts have shifted from South America to Middle-Eastern countries."

He taps another chart, which lists the countries affected over the past three years. "Over the past few years, threats have increased by over fifty percent, and the number of actual jihadists has doubled."

"Look here." I point to one statistic. "The attacks occurring in the United States relate to hacker attacks." Does he notice the relief in my voice?

"Except for Oklahoma City, which was homegrown, and the Boston Marathon attack. And of course 9/11. But yes, for now, most attacks are computer related. But look at this chart on threat levels," he warns me. "Many of those joining the jihadists currently hold United States passports. And they'll be fighting with weapons our army has left in their countries."

He scowls at the screen, as if he could wish away this nightmare scenario.

He can't. None of us can. All we can do is prepare for the worst. It looks like he's figured this out too.

"Your research is impeccable."

"Mr. Karman showed us a few tricks on how to best utilize the Internet for research. He can find anything. He also teaches Computer Science. I whizzed through Java and C++. Right now, I'm learning Ruby on Rails."

"Wow, Jeff, that's pretty heady stuff!"

"So far, I'm the only one that gets it." Jeff ducks his head, proud and embarrassed at the same time.

Just then, Trisha runs into the room and collapses on the floor. "Mommy, it's time—remember?"

I shake my head. "Remind me again, crazy little one?"

She slaps her hands on her cheeks. "How could you forget? You're going to help me with my Daisy Scout project!"

I glance at my watch. "But I have to pick up Mary from school." Suddenly an idea comes to me. I squeeze Jeff's shoulder. "Jeff, what do you say to helping Trisha awhile, just until I get back?"

He frowns first at Trisha, then at me. "Well…okay. As long as it's not too girly. What do I have to do?"

"Frankly, it's a wonderful lesson in wilderness survival. Your sister needs to identify edible plants, and create a sample box of them. She has a book that describes every plant on the list. Several of them can be found in my herb garden, out back. All you have to do is to hang with Trisha as she finds the right ones, then watch her as she snips off a leaf or two. Make sure she doesn't eat them until I get home, so that I can confirm she's on the right track. This weekend, we'll take a walk in the woods behind Hilldale Park, where we should be able to find the rest of them."

He nods. "Okay, sure."

Trisha squeals as she gives her big brother a hug. Jeff flinches. I know him well enough to realize that his first instinct is to swat her away, but then his face softens and he gives Trisha a swift kiss. Jeff has learned the hard way that we must cherish those who love and adore us.

To justify his change of heart, he shrugs, adding, "Besides, knowing that stuff will come in handy for me too."

"Why do you say that?" I ask.

He taps the computer screen with a finger. "Based on these statistics, so long fast food. I'm staying away from malls."

I tousle his hair. "Why is that, my love?"

He shrugs. "I never want to be in the wrong place at the wrong time again in my life."

I'm glad he turns back to the computer before he sees me wince. It pains me to think that he'll never feel totally safe again.

I have to get my family to focus on living life to the fullest.

The sooner, the better.

I'M ARRIVING LATE ENOUGH AT HILLDALE HIGH SCHOOL THAT the lacrosse team's practice should be over by now. If so, our semi-permanent houseguest, Evan Martin, can also catch a ride home with Mary and me.

I park my SUV in the lot closest to the school's gym. Mary will be inside, where the girl's junior varsity basketball team is practicing before the varsity team takes its place.

I'm about to walk in when I see Evan on the field adjacent to the gym, where the lacrosse team is practicing. I walk over to the practically empty bleachers and take a seat on the first row, so that I can watch the last few moments of the scrimmage. My timing couldn't be more perfect. Just at that moment Evan spins off a defender, catches a pass on the run, and sticks it in the net.

The only other people on the bleachers are three girls who are bunched together on the top row. Evan's maneuver elicits ear-piercing squeals from this ad hoc cheering squad who then lapse into a cacophony of giggles.

"Oh, my God! He's *sooooo* awesome!" one of the girls exclaims with a trill of high-pitched giggles.

Hearing this, I fight the urge to turn around.

"I think I had an orgasm," another moans.

Another girl snorts like a horse in heat. "I hate to prick your fantasy, but he's crushing on a sophomore."

"*Nooooooo!*" groans Easy to Orgasm. "What a waste! Who is she? Maybe we can make her life miserable."

"Her name is Mary Stone," says Giggles.

I sit up straight. It's all I can do to keep my eyes on the field.

"Never heard of her, so she can't be much competition," Easy to Orgasm sniffs.

"Sure you have," Snorter insists. "Her father abandoned her family to become a terrorist. After a few years, her mother had some guy move in and pretend to be her husband. To top it off, her younger brother was almost beheaded on television."

I feel my face warm up with shame. Poor Mary! As if high school isn't hard enough: she's got to live down Carl's, Jack's, and my sins.

Easy to Orgasm chuckles. "If all that is true, getting Evan away from that little drama queen should be a piece of cake."

"Something tells me it's not her 'drama' that attracted him," Giggles says. "Did you know he moved in with her? And her mother *let him!*"

They all giggle, Snorter loudest of all. "Considering how easy her mom is—well, you know what they say: 'like mother, like daughter.'"

Giggles sighs. "You'd think he'd choose a girlfriend who

was normal, what with all the hell he's already been through."

"What do you mean by that?" Easy to Orgasm asks.

"You don't know?" Snorter exclaims. "Evan's mother went to prison for ordering a hit on his father!"

"Get *out* of here!" Easy to Orgasm groans. "Wasn't she a United States congresswoman?"

"Yes, you ninny! She's Catherine Martin. Don't you remember? She was also elected *president*," Giggles chides her. "Talk about the Mother from Hell! But he was left with a fortune—and he was included in *People*'s 'Sexiest Man Alive' lists."

"Poor little rich boy," Orgasm murmurs. "He'll need some TLC, and I'm just the girl to give it to him."

Am I shocked that the sheen of sensationalism has only added to Evan's persona? Not at all. We live in the Los Angeles 'burbs, where everyone is impressed with each other's fifteen minutes of fame—or in this case, infamy.

Just then, the lacrosse coach calls it quits. Evan scans the bleachers. Seeing me, he waves, and heads over.

The girls squeal again, and whisper furiously. Of course, they think they've finally gotten his attention.

But he leans down to give me a hug. "Hi, Mrs. Stone. Thanks for the ride home," he says with a dazzling smile.

Suddenly, Snorter realizes who I am and she gasps.

"No problem at all, Evan," I say nonchalantly, but loud enough for the girls to hear. "JV Basketball practice must be over by now. Let's go round up Mary." I stand up and turn so I can get a better view of my daughter's new nemeses. Their eyes are open wide…their mouths, even wider.

The prettiest girl nudges the others. As they rise to their feet and clamber down the rows of bleacher seats, she makes it a point to graze Evan's back as she passes him.

Instinctively, he looks at her.

She smiles innocently.

He blushes, but he also smiles back at her.

Yowch.

Lucky us, they're also heading to the gym.

Orgasm purrs, "You scored the most goals today."

Evan graces her with a smile. "Oh…thanks. Yeah well, I'm doing my best to stay off the bench. I was happy the coach had room on the team."

She takes his elbow as she moves in closer to whisper something. Whatever she says causes him to duck his head shyly. He glances back as I wave. When our eyes meet, his face turns red.

I smile and shrug so that he doesn't feel as if he's been put on the spot.

We reach the gym lobby just as the girls' JV team is heading out. Mary is still talking to her coach, Ms. Lonergan. Her face is flush from the workout. Still, she nods during her coach's pep talk, and smiles when Ms. Lonergan pats her back as a sign of dismissal.

Seeing me, Mary gives a wave, and jogs toward me. She doesn't see Giggles and Snorter making a beeline for her until it's too late. Just as Snorter trips Mary, Giggles elbows her in the back.

Mary goes down hard on her knees. She groans in pain as she rolls to one side. When she gets on her feet, she's limping.

Giggles and Snorter look back to admire their handi-work, then exchange high-fives. When Mary looks back at her attackers, their "Sorry!" rings out in a singsong duet—not in falsetto, but false nonetheless.

Orgasm frowns as Evan breaks away from her in order to help Mary. Because his back is to her, he doesn't see her petulant pout, or that her eyes have narrowed into razor-sharp slits. To save face, she shrugs and saunters over to her friends.

Mary gratefully takes Evan's arm as she staggers to her feet. She wipes away the blood on her nose as she hobbles over to me.

I force my lips into a smile. "Are you okay?"

"Yeah, sure. No problem. I guess I wasn't watching where I was going." Despite her obvious pain, she is smiling. Apparently, whatever Coach Lonergan told Mary won't be easily ruined by her new enemies, which is fine by me. "So, guess what? The coach is moving me up to Varsity! One of the guards is moving out of state, and she says I'm the best player to fill her spot."

"That's awesome!" Evan says, as he high-fives her.

I turn back toward the gym floor, where the Hilldale High School girls' varsity basketball team is being put through its paces—including Giggles, Snorter and Orgasm.

"When do you start?" I ask.

"I begin practicing with them tomorrow." She stretches

out one of her bloody knees to examine it. She chides herself with a shake of her head, then hobbles toward the exit.

I pace myself so that I'm beside her. "How many other sophomores are on the team?"

"Only one. But it'll be okay. They're a great group—really supportive of each other."

We shall see.

I turn toward Orgasm and her mean girl posse, who are huddled near the bleachers. When they realize that I'm glaring at them, their sly smiles disappear.

As it should be.

Luckily for them, I was raised with manners. Make a fool of my daughter once, shame on you. Make a fool of my daughter twice, you better head for the hills—

And don't look back.

JACK LEANS OVER ME, AND MURMURS INTO MY EAR, "YOU'RE awfully quiet tonight."

I'm naked. I lay on my stomach while he crouches over me. I could lie to him and tell him that the massage he's giving me has me relaxed, tranquil, and yearning to feel him inside of me, but sadly, only the yearning part is true.

Frankly, I don't want to ruin the moment by relaying my children's travails.

The fact that I don't answer him immediately doesn't seem to bother him. Jack has always been of the assumption that all things come to those who wait, which is why he takes his time now.

Yes, I have much to anticipate—from him. All the more reason I hate the fact that he must stop in order to warm more of the rosemary-scented massage oil between his wide palms. He doesn't speak until after he has spread it on the small of my back. Instead, he waits until he has rubbed the thick liquid into my skin—

And laughs as he watches me shiver—the tease.

But yes, it is worth the wait. For you see, because even this infinitesimal reaction encourages him to do so much more.

First, his thumbs press down on either side of my spine, while his fingers rotate in small circles, into my muscles.

Yes, this makes me sigh.

He nudges me over onto my back. I watch his eyes as he sweeps away a long strand of my hair off my forehead. They are dark with concern for me.

For this, I raise myself up on my elbows so that our lips may touch.

The taste of my mouth whets his appetite for more.

His lips make a glistening trail of kisses as they work their way from my neck to my chest. He sighs as he lifts his head slightly, in order to take my left breast in his mouth.

I moan as his tongue circles my taut nipple.

He is stiffening too.

When I take him in hand, he groans with desire. The urgency in which he lifts me by my hips and flips me onto my knees thrills me. Kneeling behind me, his palms open wide so that his fingers are spread across my bottom. They tap lightly on my haunches until I give into the urge to arch my back toward him.

He takes this as a sign that I desire him; that I yearn to have him inside me.

He knows me so well.

I guide him inside of me. As I tighten around him, he cannot help but thrust and surge and come—

But he is not alone.

Our climax is simultaneous.

He collapses over me.

I feel his heart, beating in time with my own.

Finally, he rolls to my side. Still, he cradles me, as if he never wants to let me go.

I, too, wish we could stay like this all night.

In time, though, the fog of desire clears much too quickly. In its place is the clarity of my reality:

I am still sad because my children's happiness is uncertain.

It's why the tears well up in my eyes now until they overflow, forging a wet trail down my face before rolling off the contours of my cheeks, onto Jack's chest.

Startled by their dampness, he pulls away from me. "Donna! What's wrong?"

My frustration flows out of me in a torrent of barely coherent sentences—about Jeff's fears, and Mary's potential enemies—each word punctuated with a painful sob.

Jack pats me and soothes me and holds me and kisses me until, finally, I stop.

"I can't let them be hurt again."

"You can't protect them from the experiences that will help them learn right from wrong. They have to experience life—both good and bad—in order to grow emotionally, and to mature."

"I feel helpless," I mutter.

He cuddles me in the hope that my anxiety will go away.

It will, because I am not alone. He is beside me: to share my hurt, my pain, and my fears.

In time, he falls asleep. Not me. I am still restless. I worry about mundane things. Did we lock the doors? Did we set the alarm?

Does it matter? My God, we kill bad guys for a living, usually under the most surreal circumstances. For folks like us, the real boogeymen lurk in our subconscious, undermining our confidence, and playing on our trepidations.

I'm overreacting.

In other words, I'm a mother.

And a hitwoman.

Still restless, I pull away from Jack. As I slide out of the bed, something falls to the floor: a turquoise ring box.

Ah, Tiffany.

I open it. The round, multi-faceted diamond sits high on a yellow-gold band designed to look like entwined rope.

Exquisite.

Yes, after our lovemaking would have been the ideal time to ask me to marry him.

But he didn't ask because I cried and poured out my heart about my fears for my children.

He was right to wait. Timing is everything.

The next time he tries will be the right time.

I hope.

I tuck the box beside him.

This time, when I cry, it's because I feel so blessed that we found each other, and that he loves me so dearly.

With Jack by my side, everything will be all right.

3

Bolting

If you plant vegetables too late in the season, the warmer temperatures may cause them to quickly go to flower rather than produce a food crop. There is a word for this: bolting.

Certainly you've used the word in a different context—say, when riding a horse that suddenly leaps in fear of something and runs away with you clinging on for dear life.

People bolt too. Perhaps an old boyfriend or husband walked away, leaving you in shock at his desertion at a time when you thought things between you couldn't be better.

To stop a bolting horse, don't follow your instinct to pull back on the reins with both hands. Instead, disrupt the bolter's forward momentum by exerting pressure on the rein in your dominant hand. Then set the palm and base of your other hand down on the crest of the horse's neck, just above the withers. Next, be sure to keep your heels down in your stirrups, and lean back. And finally, with brute strength, bend your elbow and lift up and back with your right hand. In this position, the bolter can't bend his neck and is momentarily unbalanced, which will force him to alter his gait and pace, and to turn. Continue to exert your rein pressure until he begins to turn in a circle. Eventually, he will stop.

Should you come across your bolting significant other, shoot him. A bullet will stop him much more quickly than jumping on his back and twisting his neck.

As for plants that are bolting, hack them down to the root, and replant at the optimum time.

In two of these cases, you'll never make the same mistake twice.

Too bad the same can't be said about relationships.

"By jove, old girl! You had a run-in with Liang Xia and lived to tell about it?" Dominic Fleming's left brow rises even with his ash blond forelock.

I shrug. "Pardon? Who is that?"

He curls a finger, beckoning me toward one of Acme's conference rooms. Besides Dominic, our tech-op Arnie Locklear is there too, as well as Jack; our mission team's field-op, Abu Nagashahi; Acme's ComInt director—Arnie's wife, Emma Honeycutt; and Acme's fearless leader, Ryan Clancy.

They hover over Arnie's chair. When I'm close enough, I see why: on Arnie's computer screen is the face of the woman who picked up Yang Cheng's Buddha figurine.

Liang Xia, I presume.

"Yep, that's our gal," I murmur.

Abu lets loose with a low whistle. "According to her dossier, she's a Chinese-American operative for the PRC—People's Republic of China. The CIA has her pegged for at least sixteen exterminations of Chinese dissidents, or their relatives, who had been granted political asylum by other governments, including the United States."

"Have we discovered what intel was being traded?" Jack asks Emma.

She frowns. "The Buddha held a microdot. It's encrypted with a number for an account in a private bank on St. Kitts and Nevis, in the name of Yu Li."

"It means 'beauty,' in Mandarin," Dominic informs us. "The most famous Yu Li was the lover of a Third Century Qin Dynasty warlord, Xiang Yu."

Ryan shakes his head. "I didn't know you spoke the language."

"I've picked up a phrase, here and there."

Jack raises a brow. "There, being…?"

Dominic shrugs. "Beijing. From one of my second wives."

I cock my head in disbelief. "Really? I never knew you were married once, let alone twice!" His choice of words gives me pause. "'One of your *second wives*?' Stop me if I'm wrong, but can't you only have one spouse at a time—first, second, or other?"

"In China, 'second wife' is an expression used to describe the most coveted ladies of the night. They are kept on retainers, for the exclusive enjoyment of their patrons. I should know. When I go to Beijing, I have two of them on call at all times." He arches at me. "Double your pleasure, double your fun, eh?"

Disgusted, I shake my head. "You truly are a man-ho, you know that?"

Jack laughs. "Or what the Chinese would call a *yín chóng*."

The smile fades from Dominic's face. "You're off yer chump, old boy! *Yín chóng* is a term of endearment, or some such."

"Nope, Jack is right. Says it right here." Arnie taps his computer screen, where he's opened a page containing the term's literal Mandarin Chinese translation.

"It can't be. My second wives call me that all the time, especially when we're in the midst of a little rumpy-pumpy..." He stops mid-sentence as the fog of narcissism lifts, finally, revealing the rock-hard truth of his paid paramours' opinions.

Everyone looks anywhere else: at their feet, the ceiling, even out the window. As for me, I scrutinize the polish on my nails.

Oh bother, a pinkie is chipped.

Ryan's gruff harrumph draws all eyes to him. "We were discussing Xia, remember? Considering that what she handed Yang Cheng, the proof we need that a bioterrorism scheme to sabotage America's food supply is already under-way, I suggest we keep to the task at hand."

Our smirks fade. Yes, we are all ears.

"The Chinese have buried the cipher text within the

photos of each postcard. Sadly, Emma's ComInt team has deciphered only two of the four cards," Ryan pauses. "But what we now know is that it involves the distribution of a super-GMO seed—that is, a genetically modified organism. The seed contains a strain of a deadly virus—something doctors call an CMV—which is associated with incurable brain cancer."

"What kind of seed?" Abu asks.

"Corn," Ryan declares, "which, as we all know, is the second largest crop grown in this country. Just last year, American farmers planted over eighty million acres of it." He sighs, as if the scope of the mission has just now hit him.

"Corn, like soy, is in practically everything," Emma murmurs. It's used as a sweetener in thousands of products, as oil, and as filler. But, thank God, it's not used in baby formula."

I know why that is foremost on her mind: she recently went through the emotional debate of whether to wean her infant Nicky from her breast milk. Right now, she is still expressing her milk. No doubt that, from what she's just learned, she'll continue to do so for quite some time.

"Do we know who has the killer seed strain?" I ask.

"Yes," Ryan answers. "The cipher team pulled up the name SeedPlenish."

"Figures," Emma sniffs. "It's the world's largest agri-chemical corporation. From what I recall, it was one of the first to hit the market with genetically modified seeds."

"Have these death seeds already been distributed?" Dominic asks.

"It doesn't look like it. But from what was written in the cipher, it might be leaving SeedPlenish in as little as seventy-two hours."

Concerned, Jack shakes his head. "So, what's the game plan, boss?"

"Acme—with you as mission leader, Jack—stops the death seeds before they ever leave the warehouse and make it into the food chain."

"And that the public never learns how close we came to a full-blown pandemic," I mutter.

"Wow," Arnie mutters. "Talk about mass chaos! People will stampede grocery stores in search of food distributed prior to this week. And no one will touch any food products made with corn."

"Except for fruit and vegetables, corn is in practically everything," I add in agreement. "Despite FDA packaging regulations, many food products contain traces of corn and are incorrectly labeled."

"Don't forget: even fields that haven't been planted with GMOs are sometimes cross-pollinated," Abu points out. "If the wind doesn't shift a few errant seeds, birds pluck the plants buds and drop them on their way to their nests."

Emma's eyes open wide. "Oh, my God! If word of this gets out, American farmers and ranchers will be financially devastated!"

"Even worse, they'll be dying, like everyone else," Arnie mutters.

"Hopefully not, if we can rope this in as quickly as possible," Ryan declares. He nods to Arnie, who clicks a button on his computer.

A photo of a corporate campus appears on Arnie's computer screen. It is comprised of a round six-story building. Like spokes, long and narrow buildings branch out from it. The entire campus is surrounded by a tall fence.

"SeedPlenish's corporate headquarters happens to be located here in the LA Metroplex—Irvine, to be exact. You'll all be going undercover there." Ryan faces Arnie. "You're assigned to the IT department, working with the Optimization Modeling group. In that position, you'll be able to scan through its marketing and distribution channels. You can also tap into the main database in order to provide the rest of the team its security coverage."

Arnie gives him a thumbs-up.

"Abu, you've been hired as a truck dispatcher," Ryan informs him. "That way, we'll be able to monitor SeedPlenish's distribution routes for its corn seed."

Abu nods.

Next, Ryan turns to Jack. "Acme Financial Services has been contracted to conduct a financial audit. You'll be heading it up. This gives you the opportunity to look for recent investment capital from Asian corporations that may be acting as a front for the payoff to SeedPlenish to put the death seed in play. You'll also help us identify which of SeedPlenish's key accounts will be tapped to put this product in play. That way, we can do an end-run as quickly as possible."

Jack nods as he takes notes.

"Dominic, your cover is that of a reporter with *The Financial Times*. You'll be doing a feature on SeedPlenish's research division—specifically, the Biotechnology team, which is headed up by Dr. Lauren Rutgers. Because the SeedPlenish public relations department has already promised to bend over backwards to get you what you need in order to score a great article in such a prestigious newspaper, she'll be at your disposal to answer any and all questions you have."

"'Bend over backwards'?" Dominic smirks. "Now, that sounds promising!"

But then he sees her profile picture in her dossier, which shows a somewhat short, mousy woman, wearing a lab coat.

Dominic winces. "Crikey! Not so easy on the eyes."

To shut him up, Emma nudges him.

"Donna, there is an opening for a file clerk to the director of SeedPlenish's Plant Breeding Laboratory. His name is Dr. Thomas Wellborne. He's renowned in the biotech field, a recipient of both the Biotech Humanitarian Award, and the Astia Life Science Innovators Award." The picture that now appears on the screen shows a balding, broad-shouldered man in his early forties. What little hair he has is already graying. He too wears a lab coat. "We need to determine the stage of cultivation for the seed strain."

"In other words, if it's still in the lab, we can stop it before it gets on a truck, and mission accomplished," I reason.

Ryan nods. "The quickest way to cripple the U.S. economy is an act of bioterrorism, which has the potential to cause mass hysteria—in this case, deaths in the millions, coupled with a possible collapse of the economy. It's not the first time such an act has been considered. The Russians have been working on an Ebola bioweapon at least since the mid-seventies. But this is just as dangerous, if not more so. Even if the victim is isolated, there is no medical cure."

"The Chinese must have coded the killer seed so that it can also track its food production and distribution. Emma's team is looking for clues of this in the postcards just in case we can't find the seeds before they leave SeedPlenish." As that sinks in, Ryan shrugs. "Maybe it's time that we break for lunch. Let's meet back here in forty-five minutes for a strategy session."

As we gather our things, Dominic hands out envelopes. "Invitations to my garden party," he proclaims. "It should be rather spiffing! The usual: tea and cakes—and p'raps something with a little more kick on the side." He smiles broadly at Jack.

"Dash it! We'll be out of town that weekend," I murmur sweetly.

His eyes narrow suspiciously. "Poppycock! How would you know that, since you've yet to open it and read the date?"

Ouch! Caught red-handed. *Processing…Processing…*

Before I can finagle my foot even deeper into my mouth, Ryan shouts, "Craig and Stone—now!"

Jack jerks me in the direction of Ryan's office.

Ryan waits until we close the door before stating, "Of course, I had to report our findings to POTUS. Obviously, he asks that we update him and Homeland Security on our mission. If we fail and it gets out into the food supply, its destruction will be nearly impossible to stop, and a public announcement will have to be made immediately." Hesitantly, Ryan adds, "POTUS asks that we provide him with mission updates, in live time. Donna, you can be his point person."

Before I can pass on the honor—something I feel I should do, especially since Jack is our mission leader—Ryan's phone rings. He picks it up, scowls, and waves us out the door.

Jack frowns, for good reason. Our opinions differ greatly regarding President Lee Chiffray.

Jack feels we can't trust him. He is also very aware that Lee is attracted to me.

Okay, perfectly understandable. Then again, I don't trust the First Lady, Babette Breck Chiffray—and not just because she flirts with Jack every chance she gets.

Time to change the subject to something more pleasant. "Want to go out and grab a sandwich?"

"Not really, especially not after what I just heard," Jack mutters.

"Me neither," I admit. "So, how do we kill our lunch time?"

He points to the BMW lot, across the street. "What say we pick out another family-friendly car?"

I feel my jaw dropping. "You mean, you're parting ways with the Jackmobile?"

He shrugs. "We've got a growing family. On carpool mornings, squeezing three of us into the Lamborghini isn't exactly fun—at least, not for me. However, Mary and Evan don't seem to mind being jostled into such close quarters."

That's all he has to say to convince me. I grab his hand and lead him toward the door. "Think we can do it in less than an hour?"

"I don't know, but I'd like to give it a try. We need to be normal, if only for an hour." His smile fades. "Well, I do, anyway."

I take his hand to lead him out the door. He's right. If only for an hour, it would be nice to forget that the future of the whole human race depends on us.

"I'm telling Ryan that I don't feel comfortable being the point person with Lee." No better time to broach the subject than while Jack has a broad smile on his face, like he does now, as we test-drive a shiny black BMW i8.

I don't think the car salesman thought Jack was serious when he told him we were taking a spin up the Pacific Coast Highway. But from the look on his crestfallen face as we tore out of the lot, I give it another ten minutes before a couple of CHiP officers are pulling us over for grand theft auto.

"You'll do no such thing!" Jack proclaims.

"Pardon?" I turn to stare at him. This certainly isn't the reaction I expected. A relieved shrug, perhaps. Or he could thank me with a kiss. Then again, considering we're going up the PCH at ninety miles an hour, maybe that's not such a great idea.

Jack prefaces his answer with a shrug. "Think about it. There's got to be some reason as to why Lee wants to keep his eye on you."

Annoyed, I whip around. "You're always blaming Lee. If you remember correctly, Ryan made the suggestion. He keeps dangling me in front of Lee—"

"Trust me, I've noticed—like some sort of sparkly door prize." Jack's right brow lifts along with a smirk. "You already know my theory: Lee isn't quite the choirboy you make him out to be."

"Must we go there, yet again?" I turn my head so that he doesn't see the heat flush that is pinking my cheeks, then I remember it's unlikely that he'll take his eyes off the road.

"You misunderstand me." Jack glances my way, but only for a second, since we're coming up fast on a van. When he dodges around it, the driver toots his horn.

"How so?"

Jack veers off onto Topanga Canyon Road. In my van, the curves would make me queasy. In the i8, it's as if we're floating at warp speed. "Granted, he practically salivates when you're within his peripheral vision—so, yes, I'd like to punch him in the face. Sadly, doing so would put me in a jail cell for the rest of my life, so I keep my cool. But, Donna, I don't think it's the only reason he wants to keep tabs on you."

"Oh?" I frown. Okay, yeah, I'm a little hurt that Jack thinks it could be anything else.

"Remember, Carl's demise didn't put the Quorum out of commission. Just this morning Emma's ComInt team finally found the connection we suspected between the Quorum and Graffias International—the banking and software conglomerate that provided the helicopter for Tatyana Zakharov's getaway to and from Damascus."

Tatyana—formerly a hard woman with Russia's foreign intelligence services, the SVR—was a part of the Quorum at the same time as Carl. She led a terrorist attack on President Chiffray here in Los Angeles, where Jeff was also taken hostage.

That earned her a shove into an empty elevator shaft. If you mess with my kids, you're going down—in her case, nineteen stories, to be exact.

So, yes, this new little tidbit is interesting. "Even if Graffias International is fronting for the Quorum, what does that have to do with Lee?"

"Didn't you once tell me that Lee has always claimed that he'd never even heard of the Quorum, or had dealings with its members prior to purchasing Jonah Breck's conglomerate?"

I nod.

Jonah was one of the billionaires who secretly funded the Quorum's acts of terrorism, and in the process enlarged his very public fortune—which, unbeknownst to his stockholders who thought they were investing in green tech start-ups and eco-friendly resorts, included a snuff porn production company and website. A power play between Jonah and Carl left one man standing: Carl, whom Jonah had hired as a security consultant.

I guess you could say it turned out to be the worst business decision of his life.

"I'd once asked Lee when and how he met Carl. He told me that after Jonah's death, Babette arranged for Carl to negotiate the deal between Breck Industries and Lee's corporation, Global World Industries," I point out.

"That's according to Lee," he smirks. "There's a sheet of paper, folded in my jacket pocket. Pull it out."

"That's what she said," I mutter, as I oblige him. The pocket is taut against his broad chest, making it harder than it would be normally.

We pass a gang of bikers on HOGs. They glance over in time to see me lean into Jack, and toot their horns. One of them shouts, "Gimme some of that too, chickee-baby!"

Instead, Jack leaves them in the dust.

"I'm glad I wasn't fishing in your pants pocket," I say wryly.

"I'm not," he murmurs.

When we reach the road's highest point, he pulls over. For a moment, we sit there, staring west. A thin ribbon of blacktop barely separates the rugged hillside from the vast and torrid Pacific Ocean.

Finally, I unfold the paper. It's a list of Graffias' board of directors from eight years ago.

Lee's name is on it.

So is the name, Jonah Breck,

"At the time, Graffias was a privately held company. It's one of the reasons why this information stayed below the radar until now," Jack reminds me.

"Obviously, Lee is not still on the board," I point out.

"Only because sitting presidents can't be associated with corporations—a conflict of interest for any elected official. In regard to POTUS, all financial assets are held in a blind trust until they are out of office." He shrugs. "But if the two men were on the board together, they must have met at some point prior to Lee purchasing Jonah's companies upon his death."

"I'll admit it looks more than coincidental. But this is eight years old, and there's a possibility their paths never crossed, especially if one or the other was on the board for only a short period of time and missed the annual meeting. And even if Lee was introduced to Breck through Graffias, it doesn't prove he knew of Jonah's affiliation with the Quorum."

"Donna, come on! Carl acted as the middleman between the Breck estate and Lee. You've got to admit that Lee's previous affiliation with Jonah and Carl—and therefore the Quorum—has always been too close for comfort."

I shake my head. "I'm sorry, Jack, but unlike you, I'm not willing to buy into the idea of Lee as one of the bad guys. Do I doubt that the Quorum has its tentacles in everything, including the highest offices of governments all over the world? Not at all. The Los Angeles hostage situation proved that. My guess is that Lee realizes this too, which is why he still needs our protection. Don't forget, Lee's secret weapon against Carl was Acme."

For good reason. As Carl's former employer, Ryan felt it was his duty to bring Carl to justice. Jack's reason was personal. He was under the assumption that it was his botched mission that caused Carl's untimely demise. Just a few weeks before, his wife, Valentina, disappeared—along with a microdot containing a code to access the secure cloud holding the names and dossiers of every Acme operative. When a street security video captured Valentina with Carl exterminating an Acme agent in Hungary, Jack put two and two together: Carl had seduced her, and trained her to be one of his operatives.

And then there's me. Hell has no fury like a wife left with three children because her husband traipsed off to be a bad guy.

Jack lets me drive back to the dealership. It's a small consolation, and I take full advantage of it by breaking all speed records.

Yes, we buy the car.

And yes, Ryan is pissed that we're late. "Lunch break was over an hour ago," he growls.

Even with Carl dead and buried at the bottom of the ocean, there is enough evil to keep Acme busy. It's time to save the world, again.

4

Prickly Thorns

The most beautiful plants in any lady's garden are her flowers. But while colorful petals and sweet scents are quick to beckon one forward, one nasty prick from a thorn can mar the memory of what should have been a joyous experience.

Remember—thorns are Mother Nature's way of protecting her plants from predators. So that those who want to admire your cuttings can do so while keeping ouchies at a minimum, follow these rules:

- *Rule #1: The best time to prune is during summer or winter months. In hot weather, it's easier to trim back new growth. In cold weather, growth is dormant. Besides, you're too busy in the spring with planting new flora. (Or burying dead bodies.)*
- *Rule #2: Make sure your shears are sharp! Pull out the sharpening tools, such as a benchstone, waterstone, or*

whetstone. The rough side of these items is perfect for filing your blades. (Or for grinding a nose out of joint.)

- *Rule #3: Thin out the oldest branches first. If it's dead, chop it away! This can be done with hand shears. However if the branch is larger than a couple inches, use a handsaw (which is also useful for the wandering fingers of untoward gentlemen who might also be described as nasty pricks).*

A BEE HAS LANDED IN MY EAR.

No—

I guess I'm dreaming.

Then why won't that damn bee *shut the hell up?*

My arm reaches out to swat it away. Yes, I smack something. From his bad-tempered grunt, I realize that I hit the side of Jack's head. Oops, wrong direction. I turn on my side and force one eye open. From the way in which it is trembling on my nightstand, I realize it's my cell phone that is buzzing—

At five-twenty in the morning.

Who in hell has the nerve to call me at this ungodly hour?

Oh, my God—Ryan. *Maybe we're too late, and the killer seeds are already out there.*

My other eye pops open in order to verify that, no, it's not Ryan calling to tell us that the world has blown up. (I know this because his Caller ID shows the name and telephone number of a local pie shop that acts as a front for Acme. It was Abu's idea, really. He sells the pies, and I make them. But due to our mission schedule, we're not exactly raking it in. Still, the pin money is always appreciated.)

Then, if not Ryan, who?

I fumble with the cell phone until it clicks on. "Hello?" I sound as if I'm talking underwater.

"Donna, dear? Did I wake you?"

"What do you think?" I croak.

"Ah, such a pity." The mock sympathy in the woman's purr is all too familiar. It's Catherine Martin—Evan's mother. "Guess what happens on Friday?"

"Um…no idea."

"Go ahead, take a wild guess," she hisses.

"What…is it Black Friday? Friday the thirteenth?"

She sighs. "You could say that. It's my birthday."

"Congratulations. Don't expect a cake with a file in it."

She laughs raucously. "I expect *my son*—you remember *—the one you stole from me, using your whore spawn daughter as bait.*"

A ray of sun slips through the slanted blinds. It's going to be another glorious California day. That being said, this is not the way I wish to spend a beautiful sunrise. "Goodbye, Catherine." Her accusations are meant as barbs to make me wince with guilt, but sorry, I'm not playing her little game.

"Wait, Donna! Don't…don't hang up!"

I don't, but only because it's the first time I've heard such desperation in my old frenemy's voice. "I…I'd like to see Evan. He's avoided me since he moved in with you."

"He's seventeen, Catherine. I can't force him to see you."

"You've got more influence over him than you're willing to admit," she insists. "If the shoe were on the other foot—"

"Don't go there, Catherine. We both know that if it were me in jail, you'd do what you could to make sure I fried."

She snickers. "Okay, I'll admit it, if I'd been President, I wouldn't have minded seeing you hang at the end of a rope. Sadly, the best they can do these days is lethal injection—not that I'm worried for myself, mind you."

"I know. Your 'get out of jail' card is already secured." Evidence that our president-elect ordered a hit on her spouse was discovered prior to her inauguration. She resigned, which gave way for Lee, the vice-president-elect, to be sworn into the highest office of the land and allow the nation to recover from the shock and awe of learning of her heinous deed. Her future reward for doing so was a pardon on his last day in office.

In other words, politics as usual.

The fact that Lee was Carl's safety pick gnaws at Jack. I find it politics as usual. Since he took office, Lee has proven to be an outstanding president, as well as a true supporter of Acme.

"I'm not out of the woods yet," Catherine insists. "Which is where you come in. As much as it annoys me to be at your mercy—both as it pertains to my son, and my life—you're the only person I can trust with both."

"What the hell do you mean by that?"

"I mean that I've got the last tidbit you need to put the Quorum to rest, once and for all. But I won't let you have it unless Evan visits me on…on my birthday." Her voice cracks.

Is it the pain from her son's abandonment? Or her desperation to say, or do, anything to see him again?

Or maybe she's testing my sympathy with her well-practiced bullshit. I have to admit, it wouldn't be the first time. "You can't play me, Catherine, so don't even try."

"I'm dead serious. Even my telling you this is putting my life on the line!"

"If that's the case, why tell me at all?"

"Trust me, I wish I didn't have to, but you're the only person who can get the message to the one person who can save me."

"If you mean Lee, don't count on it. We no longer share any mutual interests."

Her laugh verges on hysterical. "Did I say it was our illustrious president? Ha! If only I could be there, to see the look on his face when you tell him. But I plan on being long gone—with your help, of course. Trust me, Donna Stone, you'll want to hear what I have to say because it's about the Quorum. You see, the second part of this deal is that when I'm sprung, Acme comes through with a new identity for me. But I'll only talk if Evan is with you. See you at noon on Friday."

"You're crazy! There is no way in hell you're walking out of prison earlier than promised, as if none of this ever happened."

"Oh no? You better figure out a way—before it's too late

for you and your family. Because once you hear what I have to say, *no one is safe."*

Before I can say anything, I'm listening to a dial tone.

If she thinks dangling intel that puts me in front of Lee is an enticement, she's got another think coming.

Like me, Catherine Martin is a mother, first and foremost. It's why she begs to see him. It's why she's using such a desperate ploy.

But if it's something that Acme should know, Ryan will insist I go.

What if I can't convince Evan to come with me?

Jack rolls over and places his arm around my waist, drawing me close.

Despite how safe I feel in his arms, I have to leave them. SeedPlenish won't appreciate it if I'm late for my first day at work.

An even harder task at hand is convincing Evan to see his mother.

It's going to be a hell of a day.

SINCE I'M ALREADY UP, I FEEL I SHOULD TAKE ADVANTAGE OF the time difference between our two coasts and check in with Lee.

So that I don't wake anyone, I dress quietly in the bathroom, then head downstairs and out the back door. To assure I'm not overheard I climb into Mary's playhouse—well, it used to be Mary's, until she outgrew it. Then it became Jeff's hangout. These days, it's Trisha's domain.

Lee picks up on the fifth ring. "I hope you didn't get out of bed on my account." The tone of his voice is much too playful for this early in the morning.

And it's certainly too playful for a president.

As Lee should know by now, it'll get him nowhere with me.

Here's one way to drive that point home yet again. "I'm up because Catherine Martin woke me. She called with a request to see her son."

"I don't envy that boy."

I could say the same about his stepdaughter, Janie, regarding her mother, but I don't think POTUS would take too kindly to my po-mouthin' his missus. Instead, I say, "Evan's not going to be happy to hear her idea. She knows this, and decided that the best way to make him come was to enlist my aid in convincing him."

"Drama queen," he mutters under his breath. "I'd think you were the last person who would help Catherine Martin do anything."

"You're right—except for the fact that she's still the mother of someone I care deeply about. So I cut her some slack." I pause, wondering if I should say more.

Okay, yeah, why not? "She feels she has a bargaining chip to make it all worthwhile," I add.

"She's played it. I've already agreed to pardon her my very last hour in office."

"That's what I told her. Still, she claims it'll happen

earlier because her intel involves the Quorum. If she speaks out, her life will be in danger."

He's silent for a moment. "If it's something we can use to shut down the Quorum…sure, I'd reconsider an earlier release date."

"Well…" How do I put this delicately? "Don't ask me why, but she'd rather tell me than you."

He's quiet for so long that at first I think I've lost the connection. "Lee?"

"If what she says is valid and something you feel you should pass forward, I'm sure you will. I trust you, Donna, to always do the right thing."

If only I felt the same way about him. "Thanks for that, Lee." I'm glad he can't see me blushing. "Now with regard to the killer seeds, I'll be embedded in SeedPlenish, along with four other agents."

"I presume Jack will be there too."

"Yes." *Don't go there, Lee.* "Mr. President, at this point, we don't know the containment situation. If the seeds are already in the ground—or God forbid, in the food chain—"

"Donna, Acme discovered the problem. As always your agents are exemplary in the area of discovery and containment. And as soon as Acme brought it to our attention, I discussed the situation with the Secretary of Agriculture, Howard Harkness. Obviously, he's very upset about it. He's personally acting as point man. He has the FDA standing by to provide HazMat coverage in addition to search-and-seizure backup."

"Good, then." For too long of a moment, neither of us

says anything, so I guess he wants me to take the lead. "So…are you and Babette planning a trip west anytime soon?"

"Separately, perhaps." Again a pause. "Maybe you'll have dinner with me."

"Jack and I would be honored."

He's gracious enough to say, "I'll be looking forward to it."

I doubt that, but I let it slide.

Then again, Jack won't like it, either.

They can both suck it up. Sometimes a lady needs all of her admirers around her. If nothing else, it ensures she won't eat a bite.

I WALK INTO THE HOUSE. NOW THAT I'M FULLY AWAKE, I desperately need a cup of coffee. I head back into the kitchen to make a pot.

Imagine my surprise to see that Mary has beaten me to the punch.

She stands in the kitchen, downing a glass of orange juice. She is dressed in her jogging sweats, and most of her hair is pulled into a high ponytail. Tiny beads of sweat cling to the tendrils around her face.

I lean in to hug her good morning, but she holds up her hand to stop me. "I appreciate the sentiment, Mom, but you look too nice, and I'm too sweaty."

I laugh as I model my prim suit for her. After earning her

thumbs-up, I ask, "And why, pray tell, are you up so early, my sleeping beauty?"

She bends a leg behind her back and pulls it tight with her hand—one of her many stretches after jogging. "I don't have gym class today, so I wanted to get in a run before school. That way, I'll be pumped before basketball practice."

"Impressive," I assure her. "I'm sure you'll wow your new teammates."

"I hope so! I'm certainly going to do what I can to pull my weight. They'll expect me to, since we're ranked number two in our division. That's thanks to our top scorer, Sara Lowell. The team is practically built around her."

"Which one is Sara?" I ask.

Mary opens her cell phone and clicks onto a web browser. A few more clicks and we're looking at the school's webpage for the girls' varsity basketball team. She points to a girl standing center, on the front row:

Oh boy. It's Orgasm.

"What do you know about her?" I ask.

"Not too much. Juniors rarely mix with sophomores. They prefer to hang with seniors, if they can."

"I hope…" I don't know how to put this delicately. "I hope they treat you with respect."

Mary shrugs. "It's like most things in life, I guess. I'll have to earn it."

"I think you have. I don't just mean your hard work on Hilldale High's junior varsity squad, Mary."

She nods. She knows what I mean. She took the news that Jack wasn't really her father pretty hard, and the news that her real father, Carl, was a traitor to his country even harder. Besides the mixed emotions toward Jack and me for living this lie for the past few years, she's also had to endure the taunts of her classmates for Carl's acts of violence and cowardice.

Her brother's brush with death at the hands of Islamic terrorists put so much into perspective.

A little sweat can't come between a mother and her daughter. As I wrap her in my arms, I whisper, "I'm proud of you, Mary."

"I know, Mom." She kisses my cheek. "And I also know there were times when I should have trusted you to do what was right for all of us. Thank you for bearing with me—and for forgiving me for being angry at you."

I bow my head. "'Every experience, even the tragic ones, are an opportunity to grow stronger." I'd learned that first with my own mother's death, then with my father's, then through my marriage to Carl. And yet, I want to spare my daughter any more pain.

She doesn't deserve the cruelty Sara may have in store for her. "Mary, should something happen that makes you at all uncomfortable in your place on the team, don't feel you have to stick it out."

She looks up at me, curious. "Why would you say that?"

I shrug. "Things don't always work out the way we want. The varsity team seems so—so *competitive*. By that, I don't mean just against their rivals, but amongst themselves too. You're there to do your best, yes. But you're also there to have fun. When you forget that, it's easy to lose perspective."

"I won't, Mom, I promise. Since the news came out about my father, I'm just happy to be accepted to anything at all." Her smile fades. "I just…I just want to be *normal* again."

She will never be that.

She will always be extraordinary.

I keep the smile on my face until she's halfway up the stairs.

To keep my mind off of what I can't control, I pull out eggs, milk, and bread for my brood, who seem to be stirring upstairs.

Maybe when Sara and her friends know Mary better, they'll change their minds about trying to make her miserable.

Or live to regret doing so.

THIS MORNING, I'VE ADDED STEAK TO THE EGGS FOR BREAKFAST. It's not just Mary who needs stamina for a long day ahead.

Evan clomps down the stairs with Jeff on his heels and Trisha on his shoulders. She carries a three-ring binder holding her plant samples, each one pressed between two pieces of wax paper.

A big brother is just what Jeff and Trisha need in their lives right now. And considering what Evan has been through, no doubt having their adoration gives him some-thing as well—say, self-respect after a year of living shamefully. Humanity rails against the sins of the father, but Evan is living proof that the sins of the mother can ruin a life too—but only if it kills all love.

With all the love surrounding him now, he'll weather this emotional tsunami.

Still, he must deal with his mother's request one way or another. I'll break the news to him on the way to school.

"—and this is dill…and this is clover…and this is wild *athparagus*!" Trisha's pronunciation of her plant collection is garbled between mouthfuls of buttered toast.

While the kids roar with laughter, I break the news to Jack that we're swapping carpool duty.

He almost chokes on a piece of steak. When he recovers, he grumbles, "Are you crazy? But—but Mary and Evan were looking forward to me driving them to school in the i8!"

I raise a brow. "What you mean to say is that you were looking forward to wowing them and all their friends with your new ride. Well, too bad. What I have to do is much more important than you reliving your glory days as big man on campus."

"I just don't know if I can take the Terrible Two this early in the morning." He's referring to Jeff's carpool buddies, the always-clueless Morton Smith, and the ever-conniving Cheever Bing. "On second thought, maybe it's best that we're switching cars. Between the two of them, they'd kill that wonderful new car smell before we got to school."

"I'll gladly trade you for what I have to do instead: break the news to Evan that his mother has requested that he see her on her birthday. She was the call that came in at five this morning."

Jack snorts. "That's Catherine for you, always considerate." With a shrug he adds, "Evan is almost seventeen. It's his decision to make."

"I told her that, in no uncertain words. However,"—I hesitate because I don't feel comfortable with what I know Jack should hear—"Catherine dangled a carrot. If not for Evan, for Acme, anyway."

"Oh yeah? What is it?"

"She claims she's got something on the Quorum that will put it out of business for good."

Jack puts down his fork. By the look on his face, he's lost his appetite. "Do you believe her?"

"Well…there was a desperation in Catherine's voice that I've never heard before. Whether it was there for Evan or because she fears for her life is hard to say. But we both know that what I think doesn't matter. Ryan will also have to weigh in on this."

"That's a no-brainer. Like us, he'd like the Quorum dead and buried once and for all."

I nod. "Okay, then. I'll use her enticement as a last ditch effort. Hopefully, it won't come to that."

Wishful thinking. We both know it.

I straighten his tie. He leans in for a kiss.

All talk amongst the children freezes, as if a bomb just went off. Trisha and Jeff are awed. Mary and Evan are mortified.

They'll grow out of it. Random acts of love and adoration should never embarrass us. Life is much too short for that.

Finally, I pronounce, "Show's over! Grab your gear and let's get moving."

The kids grumble—not because they're still enthralled, but because they'll arrive earlier than usual, by about twenty minutes. I've planned this on purpose, so that I have enough time with Evan to break the news to him.

Hopefully, I won't be breaking his heart again too.

MY FIRST DROP-OFF IS TRISHA. WHEN WE PULL UP TO HILLDALE Elementary, four other members of her Daisy Scouts troop are there to greet her. As they run off giggling, their troop leader, Lori Sloan, waves and strolls my way. Like her daughter, she is rail thin, with hair the color of copper, and a spray of freckles across her heart-shaped face. "Donna, so glad I caught you! I just want to remind you that this is the last day of the troop's cookie sales."

"True me, Trisha is on it. She's already sold fifty boxes. She's hit up the neighbors so many times that they now cower behind their curtains when their doorbells ring."

Lori laughs. "The girls are so excited. Last year, the Hilldale troop came in first place in the state for the number of boxes sold. They're bound and determined to beat their own record."

"By the way, if you need help tallying the sales, feel free to give me a call."

My offer earns me an even wider smile. "Thanks, and yes, I'll certainly take you up on that." She rolls her eyes. "Some of the other moms think Daisy Scouts is a drop-off service. Frankly, they don't understand how much fun they're missing when they bow out of some of our wonderful projects and field trips. It's all about making memories, isn't it?"

She waves as I drive off. She also has a daughter in the fourth grade, and twin fifth-grade boys. Both of her girls take ballet, and all four of her children are on the swim team. In other words, she practically lives at the school. I don't know how she does it.

Evan rock-scissors-papered his way into riding shotgun. Mary doesn't mind. Now that Trisha is gone, she can spread out on the leather back seat, like a diva on the way to some glamorous red carpet. Soon, though, she sticks her head between the front seats in order to regale us with tidbits about her new team.

"Did you know that they've never dropped below second place in our region, and that at least three players always make the county all-star team?"

I turned just in time to catch Evan rolling his eyes. "Let me guess: Sara and her two foot soldiers, Tara and Cara."

Mary taps him on the head. "You act as if you don't like them."

He shrinks in his seat. "The jury is still out. From what I can see, they can be pretty darn nasty."

"Oh yeah?" she asks. "In what way?"

"To the other girls. I see it all the time." He hesitates. "And for that matter, to guys too."

I keep my mouth shut. It's much better for Evan to make my point.

Mary leans back. She doesn't know what to make of his warning. Frankly, I hope she takes it to heart. But by the way in which she leaps out of the car as I screech to a stop, it's obvious that it's the last thing she cares to hear. "Jack is doing pick-up!" I shout after her.

Evan is about to hop out too, when I pull him back. "By the way, your mother's birthday is next Friday."

He frowns. "What of it?"

"She called. She'd love to see you."

"I can't. Our lacrosse team is in the semi-finals."

"Evan, I know it's hard for you to forgive her. But still—"

He shakes his head adamantly. "I can't. It's…it's too soon."

"Prison is not a pretty place. For all you know, it may be the last time."

He takes a deep breath. "I can barely remember the last time I was with my dad. All I remember is that he looked so sad, and that he was determined to talk to my mother alone —really, to have it out with her. He must have asked her a billion times, but there were always so many people swarming around—Mother's campaign entourage. The truth was that she was afraid to be alone with him—afraid to look him in the eye. Now I know why."

He stares out the car window. Waves of students pass us —chattering, giggling, and whispering, seemingly without a care in the world. They are unlike Evan, who must carry the weight of his mother's misdeeds for the rest of his life.

My words stick in my throat, but I must say them. "Evan, your mother claims to have some vital intel on the terrorists who were financing her campaign. But the only way she'll come clean with it is if you go to see her on Friday."

His head twists in my direction. His eyes are shadowed by disbelief. "She told you that? She's lying! She's conning you!"

"She may be, but we can't take that chance. Please, just think about it."

He nods, but from the tilt of his chin, I can tell it's a long shot.

I don't know what I'll tell Ryan.

The good news is that I don't have to face him immediately. Right now, the most important task in the world is finding those bad seeds.

If we fail at our mission, Evan's decision may come too late anyway.

5

Ridding Your Garden of Pests Organically

Any insect or animal that invades your garden and eats, or worse yet, kills, your prized flowers and vegetables is a pest.

Pests should be deterred at all costs, except for that of your plants' lives, and your own. That being said, consider extermination methods that aren't toxic to your garden, let alone those you love.

For example, bury an empty tuna can in dirt up to its rim, then fill with beer. Slugs get a hangover, fall asleep, and drown. (Yes, I can imagine it reminds you of your sorority days.) Also, to eradicate earwigs, leave newspaper scattered in the yard, to collect the morning dew. These bugs like to crawl under the damp pages, which you can just roll up and throw in the trash. Aphids hate citrus. Steep an orange or lemon rind in scalding water overnight, and by morning your citrus juice can be poured into a spray bottle. Squirt the tops and bottoms of leaves, and problem solved!

Ridding your home of human pests in an environmentally safe way is just as easy. In that regard, your garden comes in quite handy, since it's filled with all sorts of drugs or poisons. One prick with a rosary pea, and you're assured that your nosy neighbor's next sleep will be eternal. A sip of tea laced with oleander and those salesmen who ring your doorbell will soon be pushing up daisies.

(Helpful hint: corpses make great fertilizer!)

ALL OF SEEDPLENISH'S NEW EMPLOYEES MUST SIT THROUGH A human resources video that explains what the company does, and how it does it.

The public version, anyway.

There are sixty others in the auditorium with me, including Jack, Abu, and Arnie. Most of them stare at the wall-sized screen in front of us, where a thirty-something actress and actor—pretending to be farmers, but wearing jeans much too new, and blue oxford shirts much too creased —espouse SeedPlenish's sales pitch: from-seed-to-store, the journey presents a well-fed world with folksy phrases that are sure to make us all drink the corn syrup-laced Kool-Aid.

We are also told that genetically modified seeds aren't just the future, but the present (check), and that "traited" (that is, GMO or biotechnically-altered) seeds are safe to use. (I hold myself back from shouting at the top of my lungs "Not true about at least one particular corn seed, so beware!")

Arnie's eyes are elsewhere: specifically on the screen of his laptop. Now that he's armed with an employee ID, he has easily hacked into SeedPlenish's secure cloud. Right now, he's busy downloading its sales and seed distribution files. He's also forwarding the company's files and correspondence between its banking and investment partners to Jack.

As for me, he's sent me the personnel file on my new boss, Dr. Wellborne. He has two undergraduate degrees, not to mention masters and doctoral degrees, all from Stanford, in various fields: Biology, Genetics, and Bioengineering.

Ms. Conover, SeedPlenish's quote-unquote "in-house corporate evangelist" (CorporateSpeak for Human Resources Director), roams between the aisles of chairs, like a nun on the hunt for students passing smutty notes. I've just finished reading Dr. Wellborne's bio when I realize she's only a few feet away from me. I barely have time to swipe to a different screen on my iPad. Unfortunately, it's one of a Jimmy Fallon's now-classic late night video in which he's in a lip-sync battle with Joseph Gordon Levitt and Stephen Merchant.

Note to self: no more surfing the Web on Acme-issued devices.

As Stephen twerks to Beyonce's incomparable lyrics, "*If you liked it then you should have put a ring on it—*" Ms. Conover's brow disappears in the thick recesses of her razor-straight bangs. "Excuse me, Ms. Stone, I have to ask: do you think that you're giving me and your colleagues a full 110 percent right now?"

"Um…Sorry! I just…it was a mistake." I slam the iPad face down on the table in front of me. Finding the MUTE button would have been wiser, considering the snickers when Beyonce's anthem crescendos into the chorus *"All the single ladies—"*

Jack reaches over and does the honors. Neither he nor I miss the look on Ms. Conover's face when he honors her with his dazzling smile.

No surprise, she forgets she was scolding me, let alone that I'm even here.

When she's finally able to break his spell, she throws her arms wide, as if to embrace everyone in the room. "Ms. Stone, your co-workers are about to embark on a marvelous journey, up SeedPlenish's strategic ladder. As they climb each glorious step, they'll be met with promotions, raises, stock options…" She pauses at the thought. Then, as if she's finally seen the light, she leans in and hisses, "So do yourself a favor—*don't get left behind.*"

As I look around, I'm met with anxious frowns.

And one smirk—Jack's, of course.

I scratch my forehead with my middle finger. Jack takes the hint.

He asks, "Excuse me, Ms. Conover, is it lunch time?" The question sounds innocent enough—if you didn't notice that it came with a naughty grin.

"Why…um, yes, it is." She smiles back, then claps her hands at the rest of us. "The company cafeteria is to the left and down the hall. You have one hour. Please take your campus maps and find your way to your department, where your superiors are waiting to brief you on your new duties, once you return."

Other than a free lunch, I hope he gets something out of her.

Or maybe not. If anyone knows the best place to (in a full bastardization of CorporateSpeak) let him climb her strategic ladder in order to drill down 110-percent, it's got to be the corporate evangelist.

"So, you're the new girl...woman...whatever." Dr. Thomas Wellborne must like what he sees because he quits smacking his gum in order to give me the once-over. If he ever resembled the profile photo on the company website, it was at least fifteen years, forty pounds, and a full head of hair ago.

"Donna will do," I assure him.

"Okay, Donna it is." He shrugs as he leans in—a bit too close, if you ask me—in order to shake my hand.

When I take a step back, he gets the message: *Down, boy...man...whatever.*

"How good are you at burying paperwork?" He nods toward my new desk, which is located in a large filing room in the building housing the R&D department. There is a five-hundred-acre cornfield between it and the rest of the company's corporate campus. Forget being as high as an elephant's eye. The twenty-foot corn stalks beyond the room's two-story window undulate under a gentle breeze like a bamboo forest.

I look down at the mess. "Got a shovel?"

Frankly, a wind not much stiffer than the one blowing outside the window is all it would take for the mountain of folders and binders to begin the inevitable avalanche.

He shrugs. "Hey, don't blame me. My past two assistants left a lot to be desired. One was out in six months. The last little lady did her one better: one week and out. Jesus, you'd think I was some sort of slave driver, or an abusive boyfriend or something!" Hoping to entice me, he raises his bushy brows twice, then licks his lips, as if I'm a pork chop.

When I don't take the hint, he reaches beyond me for a file. It grazes my breast as he opens it and scans the first sheet. "Just what I thought! She never even got around to last quarter's results. Why don't you start with this pile of folders? Each batch of seeds is numbered. My field researchers assess our latest test seeds by notating the growth of each stalk."

"I'm surprised this wasn't done by computer."

He chuckles. "Even iPad screens aren't easy to read in bright sunlight. Which is where she came—and now, you *come*…in." This lame pun is his lame excuse to keep leering at me. "You'll scan these sheets on that thing." He slaps the desktop copier on the credenza. "That way, the data ends up where all pertinent divisions of SeedPlenish can access it: research, sales, marketing, even accounting." He's under the impression that leaning against the wall makes him look sexier.

Losing his potbelly would be a better move. You'd think

he'd figure this out when his gut knocks a couple of the folders onto the floor.

"It's a fairly big job. I better get to work." I bend quickly to catch yet another falling folder.

Bad move by me. The next thing I know, his hand is cupping my ass.

Worse move by him, because the next thing he knows is that I'm twisting his nuts.

He yelps, but gets the lay of the land and skedaddles back down to the first floor where the rest of the R&D staff are holed up, playing mad scientist with the genetic makeup of God's bounty.

Good riddance. I'm not here to bury dead files that no one will ever read, or to be a plaything to some horny clown in a lab coat. I'm here to learn whether the killer seeds are already out the door.

I stare out the window. Twenty-eight silos are lined up on the north side of the field, identical aluminum sentries reflecting bright rays in full sunlight. I have to shield my eyes in order to look at them. They stand at least thirty feet tall, and ladders go up one side. They are elevated, and their bottoms are coned so that the bags of dry corn kernels held within can be funneled into SeedPlenish's delivery trucks. Right now, bags are being dropped from Silo Number 18.

Which one contains the killer seeds?

By jove, I think I've found them—thanks to Jilly, whomever she is.

She left in such a hurry that she didn't even take the time to clean out her desk. A month-old ticket to a San Francisco Giants–Los Angeles Dodgers game is in one of the drawers, as well as an autographed photo of Buster Posey.

I guess we know which team she roots for. But, obviously, she didn't make the game, or the ticket wouldn't still be here.

Dr. Wellborne was stupid to leave me her computer, especially since SeedPlenish's tech personnel haven't ditched her old password. First, I try *BusterPosey*. No luck. Then *Buster*, then *Posey*. Both dead ends.

I use my cell to call Arnie. "I'm trying to hack my predecessor's computer. From what I can tell, she's a baseball fan —specifically of the SF Giants' Buster Posey. I've tried the name in various combinations, but no luck."

"Didn't you read your manual? For example, the password has to be alpha-numeric."

Duh.

"Just a wild guess, but why don't you try the name, 'Buster,' with his team number?"

I type *Buster28*. "Bingo," I murmur.

"Link me in," Arnie suggests. It's a good idea to allow his employee ID to access it as well, so that he can see what I'm seeing, and perhaps pick up on other clues throughout all her stored data.

We roll through her emails. At first, the ones to and from

Dr. Wellborne are all business, then become flirtatious, and, finally, all pleasure—

Until the last week of her employment. For some reason, the tone is now stilted and distant.

The last email between them comes from her. It reads, simply:

You lied. It hurt.

"She is—or was—a Thomas Wellborne fan girl—at least, at first," I murmur. A renowned scientist as a notch on your belt? To each her own, I guess."

"Wow, wow, wow," Arnie murmurs excitedly. "Jackpot!"

A file pops up on my screen, entitled, *Strain v.101313.*

"How do you know this is it?" I ask.

"Because she copied it from his secure cloud."

"I wonder how she figured out his password," I mutter out loud.

"She knew him well enough, I guess. By the way, it's *AssMan1.*"

Ouch. Yep, that hurts.

"Apparently, she got her revenge. This file has everything: his correspondence with an entity he refers to as BIG PAY DAY, in which he puts out feelers for its interest in what he calls 'the Exodus Strain, 22:6.' There is also a response in the affirmative, along with confirmation of a one billion-dollar payoff, placed in a Cayman Islands bank account."

"'*Exodus?*' That's a book in the Old Testament of the

Bible." A thought hits me. "Hey do me a favor and look up verse 22:6."

I hear a few clicks. "Oh, yeah, this is it," he finally says. "It's a real toe-tapper too. Listen to this: '*If fire break out, and catch in thorns, so that the stacks of corn, or the standing corn, or the field, be consumed therewith; he that kindled the fire shall surely make restitution.*' Well, I guess we now know who's been quote-unquote kindling the fire."

"Poor choice of words, but I hear you. If this Jilly person took off, something tells me it's because things got too hot for her to hang around, no pun intended," I say with a sigh. "Arnie, is there any indication where the seeds were—or hopefully, are—being stored?"

"My guess is that Wellborne keeps them within reach, and within sight. The R&D department's organizational chart shows that half of SeedPlenish's silos hold dry corn kernels, and the other half hold bags of fresh corn."

"At least we now know which half to investigate."

"That would be Silos Fifteen through Twenty-Eight."

"Is there any way to narrow it down even more?" I ask.

He's silent as he taps away. Finally, he says, "Let me work on it for a while. By the way, I've duplicated what we have here, and uploaded it into the Acme cloud, so that you and Emma's ComInt team can also scan for clues. Keep your cell phone handy in case we come up with anything, okay?"

"Will do. In the meantime, text Ryan to put a tap and a tracer on Dr. Wellborne's phones—home, office, and cell. If we get lucky, he may lead us to the Exodus seeds."

I spend the rest of the afternoon going through the office,

to see if Jilly planted some clue as to which silo contains the Exodus strain, but I find nothing.

Since I worked through my lunch hour, I clock out an hour early. From here to home still puts me in I-405 traffic, but at least I'll get to Hilldale in time to pick up Trisha and Jeff.

I text Jack to give him the great news that I'll be couriering Cheever and Morton. Only after I hit SEND do I remember that I'll be doing it in the new Jackmobile.

Oh well, goodbye to that wonderful new car smell.

THE FIRST MISTAKE CHEEVER BING MAKES IN JACK'S NEW BMW is to let loose with a burp. "Tacos," he says as a way of apology. "Gotta love 'em."

His next faux pas is to jump in the front passenger seat. "I call shotgun!" he crows.

I shake my head. "No, no, no—out! That's where Trisha sits when we pick her up."

"But—but I called shotgun!"

"You can call a cab for all I care. Better yet, if you want to lose those taco love handles, walk home."

He shuts up. But instead of opening the door, he climbs over the front seat into the back.

"I call window!" He shoves Morton Smith toward the middle. Morton shoves back.

I'll be damned if I'm going to play Margaret Dumont to

their Groucho-Chico shenanigans. "Jeff, in the middle, please."

"But, Mom, today was taco day."

Note to self: look at middle school lunchroom menu before committing to carpooling—especially in the new car. Oh well, too late now.

Cheever waits until I pull onto the road before making his third mistake: slapping Jeff on the head. "Hey, what's the big idea, turning in a forty-page paper for Current Events class?"

"Yeah," Morton growls. "You made the rest of us look bad."

Jeff shrugs. "If the shoe fits."

"Terrorists don't wear shoes. They wear sandals." Cheever says smugly.

Morton stares at him, confused. "That's stupid! I wear sandals, and I'm not a terrorist."

"You're right. You're just a moron." Cheever reaches over to Jeff to pinch him. "I'm talking about the real ones, you moron—you know, like in the Middle East."

"You're both morons," Jeff counters. "Terrorism has taken place all over the world, Germany, Ireland, Africa, South America, even here in the United States—you name it. And from all nationalities too. Pay attention in History class, why don't you?"

"Yeah?" Cheever taunts him. "Well, you haven't noticed it here in Hilldale—right under your own nose too."

I look at Jeff in the rearview mirror. As I suspect, his eyes open wide with concern. "What the heck are you talking about?"

"I'm talking about that teacher you're always sucking up to: Mr. Karman."

"You're nuts," Jeff snorts.

"No, I'm not! I looked in his window during lunchtime. He was on his hands and knees, on a blanket, mumbling something—just like they do in the terrorist movies. I asked my mom, and she says that means he's a muslin, which means he's an Arab, which means he's probably a terrorist," Cheever says smugly.

"The word is 'Muslim,' not 'muslin,' which just so happens to be a fabric, not a religion," I point out. "And by the way, not all Muslims are Arabic. And whereas it's the dominant religion in Arabia and all of the Middle East, this can also be said about fourteen countries in Africa, most of Indonesia, some of Russia, and a few small countries in South America. And, guess what? Two million United States citizens are Muslim as well."

"Why do you know so much about it?" Cheever asks. "Is it 'cause your old man was a terrorist?"

I slide the car to the curb and turn off the engine. "The point I'm trying to make, Cheever, is that one doesn't have to be Arabic to be a terrorist. Or Muslim, either. You can be Methodist, or Catholic, or even an Atheist! To be a terrorist, all one has to 'be' is willing to hurt or kill others to make one's point—"

Jeff's head is down.

Oh hell, I've gone too far.

"Which 'one'?" Morton asks.

"Any*one*!" Jeff yells. "That's the point—any*one* can be a terrorist!"

The next thing I know, he's climbing over Morton to get out of the car. Slamming the door, he trots off.

At least he's going in the direction of the house.

I turn to Cheever. "Mr. Karman hasn't hurt anyone. Your mother is wrong—not to mention hurtful, and unnecessarily cruel."

"No? Well, at least she hasn't killed anyone—*like you have*."

I start the car. I'd give the little brat the ride of his life, except for the fact that I'm afraid he'd pee his pants, and this is Jack's new car, after all.

The only good to come out of my so-called conversation with Cheever is that the rest of the ride to Trisha's school and then home is made in silence.

I've just walked into the house with Trisha when I get a text from Evan. It reads *We're stranded.*

Jack hasn't yet left SeedPlenish? I guess he's been detained.

Jeff seems to have calmed down. He gives me a hug and nods absentmindedly when I ask him to watch Trisha while I go get his sister from practice.

On top of his knapsack is his research paper. The grade: A+++.

I can see why. The finishing touches included maps, PowerPoint organizational charts, timelines, and pictographs of recent attacks.

If I showed it to Ryan, he'd hire him on the spot. But somehow, I don't think Ryan would let him off in the afternoon for baseball practice, so it's a nonstarter.

When I pull up in the new Jackmobile, Mary and Evan are standing with Sara, Cara and Tara. Mary runs over to me and asks, "Mom, would you mind if they come home with us? Sara is third-year French. She wants to show me some tricks to ace my exam."

Sara leans over her shoulder. "We want to make sure she keeps up her grades so that she can stay on the team."

I'll just bet.

I shrug. "Sure, hop in."

"It's not what you think," Jack insists when, finally, he gets home. "Trust me, I was on a reconnaissance mission."

"Thought so. With the in-house evangelist, I presume."

"If it's any consolation, it was one drink and out."

"I hope you slipped her a truth serum."

"I didn't need to. All it took was a Mai Tai."

I shake my head. "Why am I not surprised? And what golden nuggets did you glean?"

"Tammy claims that—"

"Tammy? How sweet that the two of you are already on a first name basis."

"I'd be more flattered if you were truly jealous."

"And I'd be truly jealous if I thought she was capable of saying anything that didn't come out of the company handbook. So, did she?"

"Oh, I'll say she did." Whatever it was puts a grin on his face. "But as far as this case is concerned, she did let go with one interesting fact: Wellborne has been passed over for promotion to company president twice, which gives him a possible motive for cashing in on the killer seed."

"I wouldn't doubt it. Considering his touchy-feely management technique, I'm surprised they haven't fired his sorry ass by now."

"When Tammy told me about her own tickle-and-slap sessions with him, I asked the same question. She claims that he's too valuable of a scientist. Besides, he knows where all the bodies are buried."

"He's a letch, no doubt about it. He actually admitted that his last two assistants didn't last even a year in the position. I may have stumbled onto the paper trail on the killer seeds, but I'm not sure. His last assistant left the files a mess. She may have done it on purpose."

"What was her name?"

"Jilly McIntosh. Maybe, by now, Arnie has hacked her personnel file and passed it forward to Emma to look for any red flags—you know, see if her placement in the department was legitimate, including her next place of employment—"

I pause, because it sounds as if a herd of elephants are coming down the stairs, but it's only Mary with her new entourage.

Evan is heading in the opposite direction—from the kitchen, where he's been focusing on his homework, to his room, which is the bonus room over the garage. When Sara passes him, she grazes against him, on purpose. He ignores her not-so-subtle attempt to get his attention. She tosses her head angrily as she flounces into the kitchen with the other girls.

Jack's head swivels back in my direction. When his brow goes up, so do my hands, as if they could wield off his amused glance. "Mary begged me to give them a lift. She claimed they want to help her with her French homework."

"Are you sure they didn't mean Evan?"

"From all the seductive naughty talk aimed his way, no doubt about it."

He shakes his head. "They're using her."

"I know it, and you know it. Even Evan knows it. But Mary hasn't figured that out yet."

"You can't be the one to burst her bubble," he warns me.

"I have to. If those little witches pop it first, it'll hurt a hell of a lot more."

"Sadly, you're right, on both counts." He kisses my forehead. "Go for it, but don't be surprised if she doesn't listen to you. Mary has to find her own path, even if the road is bumpy, or takes her off course."

Whatever else he has to say is cut off by the buzz of my

cell phone. Arnie is calling. "The shipment happens tonight, two in the morning," he says urgently.

"Do we know where?"

"No. The time was set by phone, and it was cryptic. All Wellborne said was, 'Yes, meet you there.' He must have been talking to the driver who'll be taking it where it needs to go."

"Were you able to put a trace on the driver's phone?"

"Unfortunately, it was a burner, so no. It was out on Highway 5, so I presume he was completing a run."

"Grab Abu and Dominic, and meet us at the gates to the SeedPlenish compound at midnight. We may need more manpower."

"Will do. Right before we arrive, I'll loop the webcams, so that Security never even knows we're there."

I hang up and turn to Jack. "Speaking of detours, the mission team has to take one tonight, around midnight. Wellborne is our man, and he's moving the seeds tonight."

"Why don't you call Aunt Phyllis and tell her the guest room is hers? That way, the kids are covered for the evening, and for drop-off, if need be."

We can hear the girls giggling as they tromp from the kitchen and back to the foyer. When they reach the foot of the stairs, Sara shouts, "Evan, you can't hide from us forever!"

Concerned about our reactions, Mary glances over at us. When our eyes meet, she blushes a deep red, but follows the other girls up the stairs.

Turning to Jack, I shake my head. "Enlisting Aunt Phyllis

is a great idea. And I'll tell her, quite emphatically, that there are to be no sleep-overs."

Jack rolls his eyes. "No kidding! Nothing these girls are doing with Mary even closely resembles French."

"Maybe that's the real game plan: to get Mary to flunk French, so that she's kicked off the team."

"If so, it'll be the best thing to come from this ordeal."

He's right. It's a hard lesson, but at least Mary will know the true meaning of friendship.

The minute Aunt Phyllis shows up, we're out the door.

Evan has yet to come out of his room. I can't say that I blame him.

6

Weedwacker

The Weedwacker is a wonderful lightweight device that holds a quickly rotating string, the velocity of which can cut all grass within its reach, thus assisting the avid gardener in keeping her lawn trimly clipped.

A "lady of the night" is apt to use the term as well, in reference to a client who insists on slapping her in the face with his one appendage that isn't part of a pair.

Should the former weedwacker have a run-in with the latter, we can pretty much guess the victor:

The lady.

AH, HELL. THERE ARE FOUR TRUCKS LINED UP OUTSIDE OF SILO Twenty-Two.

The loading of the Exodus seeds has already started.

Three of the trucks are already loaded with bags of seed.

Another is under a cone, being filled.

We can hear the hum of the trucks' engines. Except for the driver loading his truck, the others stand in semicircle around Dr. Wellborne, who seems to be briefing them on something. There is no moon tonight. The only light in the area comes from the trucks' headlights.

"Okay, here's the plan," Jack murmurs. "From left to right, Dominic takes Truck One, Abu takes Truck Two, I'll Take Truck Three, and Donna takes Truck Number Four. Kill the tires first. If possible, take the drivers and Dr. Wellborne alive, for further interrogation."

His instructions come too late, in regard to Truck One, anyway. As the driver hops into it and roars off down the road, Dominic runs after it.

His first two shots ping the truck. The next one sends it skidding into the cornfield. Dominic reaches the cab before the driver runs off into the field.

Before the other drivers scatter, Jack, Abu and Arnie draw their guns and round them up.

On the other hand, Thomas takes off behind the silos.

"I've got Wellborne!" I shout to Jack.

I mean, how fast can he run, really?

NOTE TO SELF: NEVER UNDERESTIMATE THE ADRENALINE RUSH that can take place in a man who realizes his capture means spending the rest of his life in a Federal penitentiary for treason and terrorism.

I take off after Thomas as fast as I can, but his head start puts him far enough away that I'd be wasting bullets if I tried to shoot him in the dark.

When we're beyond six of the silos, he starts losing steam. He stumbles to the backside of the nearest silo.

By the time I get to it, he's climbed halfway up the ladder.

My first shot whizzes past his ear. He pauses, but then goes hand-over-hand on the rungs even more quickly, until he's at the door on top of the silo.

There's nothing I can do but follow him. At least up there, he'll be cornered.

"Who are you, really?" Thomas asks. The question bounces through the silo.

"Does it matter, Thomas? Game over." I can't pinpoint him by the sound, and the inside of the silo is pitch black.

From what I can see, a three-foot catwalk spans the length of silo, but what little light there is comes in through the open door and only shows a third of it before recessing into the black abyss beyond. I draw my gun. Then slowly, I step through the doorway.

An overhead light blinds me, but I hear the door closing behind me.

And I certainly don't see the punch to the gut coming.

Damn it, my gun drops out of my hand, into the corn kernels below. As for me, I fall forward and nearly roll off the catwalk, but I catch hold just in time.

Thomas's arms reach around my waist. He heaves me up, only to slam my head into the wall before dropping me back on the catwalk. I'm too stunned to do anything but rise onto my knees.

I feel his forearm on my back, bracing my face and shoulders against the catwalk. "It's a wonderful position for a woman, almost like praying for mercy," he murmurs. I try not to shiver when he licks my ear. "Ever try anal sex?"

When I don't say anything, he takes that as a no.

"Sweet, a virgin! Okay, word of warning: I've heard it feels like a hard turd going in backward. But you'll be happy to know that it doesn't feel like that on this end. Let me tell you, the sphincter is the tightest muscle in the human body, especially when it tries its damnedest to stay closed." He laughs. "You better hope I ride you long and hard, because once I'm done with you, I'm tossing you in there."

He shoves my neck over the edge of the catwalk so that I'm staring down into it. "You won't see it in the employee video, but we've actually had a few poor guys fall off the catwalk. Everyone tries to fight their way out, but no one's made it yet. It takes five minutes, tops, before they suffocate."

He slams me back onto the catwalk. He uses his free hand to knock my knees apart. When he tries to pull down my pants, he finds my cuffs.

"Oh, my God, how nice is this?" he crows. "You brought your own play toys!"

He rips them off my belt loop, then jerks me up by my hair in order to cuff my hands in a praying position, before slamming my wrists back onto the catwalk.

I snort. "Really? Do you really believe that tiny thing of yours will reach beyond your gut?"

He smacks me hard on the backside. "You're about to find out. Giddyap, cowgirl!"

He pulls my pants down to my thighs. "Nice thong." He twists it tight. "What say I work around it? It'll give me something to look at, besides all the blood."

To ride me, he still has to pull down his pants. I can't see him, but I can hear him unbuckling his belt, but only with one hand. When he smacks me on the back with it, I flinch, but I don't groan.

Wait for it...Wait for it.

He unbuttons with one hand again, but he needs two to move the zipper.

I bear down on my forearms and release a high kick with both legs.

It catches him right in the gut.

He falls backward, on his ass. As he struggles to sit up, he gets another kick—this time, in the teeth.

It puts him flat on his back again.

I land on his chest, hard, with both knees. While he gasps for air, I take my elbows and slam his head into the catwalk. He whimpers in pain.

Suddenly, the door opens. I look up to find Jack standing

there. Seeing my hands cuffed in front of me, he shrugs. "I took a wild guess that you were all tied up."

He kneels in order to put the barrel of his gun to Thomas' forehead. "No sudden moves. No one likes brains with their cornflakes."

I get up. Jack hands me his handcuffs. "Would you like to do the honors?"

"Do you even have to ask?" I kick Thomas. "Sit up slowly, then put your hands—*behind* your back."

He knows better than to disobey. I cuff one hand, then the other. When I'm done, Jack pulls out the key and unlocks my cuffs.

"Now, get up, nice and easy, Dr. Wellborne," Jack warns him.

The bad doctor rolls to one side so that he can get onto his knees. He then rises onto one leg. When he's on both feet, he charges me—

Jack shoots.

Thomas is just inches away when the bullet pierces his back. The light goes out of his eyes. He topples forward—

Onto me.

I try to sidestep his grasp, but I can't. I flail my arms to get my balance, but I'm caught in the forward momentum of his now-dead body. We both go over the side—

A cloud of corn dust rises as Thomas slaps into it.

On the other hand, I'm dangling in mid-air, upside down, by my ankle.

"I thought you were dieting," Jack mutters as he heaves me back up onto the catwalk.

I smile. "Why mess with perfection?"

He shrugs. "You've got a point. By the way, since I'm already down on one knee, will you marry me?"

"There's a dead body below us ready to be fast-frozen in a bag of corn kernels, and who knows how many trucks of killer seeds out there on their way to who knows where. I'd say your timing is a little off."

"You have a point. Business before pleasure." He gets off his knees.

He heads out the door.

Maybe I was too hard on him. It would have been easy to just have said yes.

But no. This isn't how I envisioned his proposal would happen. Doesn't he realize that?

There will be a better time, and a better place, but first things first. When your business is saving the world, everything else has to wait. That's just the way it is.

ABU AND DOMINIC HAVE ALREADY TAKEN THE DRIVERS BACK TO Acme's holding pen.

When we get back to headquarters, Ryan is watching the camera monitor broadcasting from inside the interrogation room. "Where's Thomas?" he asks.

Jack grimaces. "Dead."

Ryan frowns. "What part of 'take him alive' wasn't clear to you two?"

I shrug. "Oh, I don't know. Maybe it's the part where he

tried to rape me, then toss my body into a silo of corn where I'd suffocate to death."

Being fluent in Ryan's grunts, I'm able to make out his apology.

"There's one bit of good news. The Acme lab rats have compared the seeds to the DNA diagram on one of the cards that was confiscated from the MSS handoff. It's a match."

"So, we have the killer seeds right here," I murmur. I shudder at the thought.

"But not for long," Ryan assures me. "The FDA is sending a security detail to pick it up and destroy it. Tomorrow, there will be a raid on SeedPlenish. The corn and seed in every silo will be searched, and every corn stalk in the research field will be tested. If it proves to be part of the Exodus strain, it will be confiscated and then destroyed as well."

"What about the drivers?" Jack asks. "Do they know anything?"

"They're being held in separate soundproof cells. They're Mexican illegals, hired by Wellborne for late night deliveries," he informs us. "They presumed you were an Immigration Service patrol, which is why they took off and ran."

"In other words, they know nothing about the seeds other than the destinations for their deliveries," I reason.

"We were able to confiscate their manifests. We can interrogate the receiving entities too," Jack adds.

"Abu and Dominic are on it, first thing tomorrow," Ryan replies. "All are Big Agra farms whose corn is distributed to food manufacturers of all kinds. Chances are they didn't know what they were getting—and wouldn't, until it was too late." He pauses to wipe the fatigue from his eyes. "Now for the bad news. Apparently, this wasn't a first run, at least for one of the drivers. He did another delivery almost two months back, to an independent farmer in Dixon, right up the road." Ryan scribbles down the address and hands it to me.

It says Clover Hill Farms. "We'll check it out now," I promise.

Ryan nods. "Good idea, since it's still dark. George is standing by, ready to take you by helicopter."

"Does the corn have any identifying marks?" Jack asks.

Ryan nods. "Its color is almost as much orange as it is yellow, and the stalks have a blue tinge to them. Also, the kernels and husks are larger than normal."

"Talk about genetically modified," I mutter.

"The one bit of good news is that this driver also rounded up the other three, so I presume it may have been the first time the Exodus strain made it out of the silo," Ryan says.

"Let's hope so," Jack mutters.

"Unfortunately, two months is just long enough to grow a field of corn, depending on the strain and the temperature conditions," I explain. "A few years back, we grew a few stalks in the back yard. It was one of Mary's fifth grade Geography projects."

"Then that crop should be ready for harvest right about now," Jack reasons, "if it hasn't been, already."

There's a knock on the door. Hearing Ryan's bark,

Emma enters, pushing a stroller where her infant son, Nicky, sleeps peacefully. Rocking it side to side, she murmurs, "I combed through Jilly McIntosh's personnel file, and did a background check as well. She's clean as a whistle: raised in Lodi, basketball star for her high school team, and earned her degree in Genetics from UC-Davis. Unfortunately, she graduated during the Great Recession. She was surviving on minimum wage jobs before she got hired at SeedPlenish. She was certainly overqualified to be a file clerk, but it paid better than anything she had before it, and at least it put her in a field where she could use her training."

"She must have thought working under Wellborne would be a dream come true. But from the correspondence I saw, it was more like a nightmare." I shudder. "So, where is she now?"

"Nowhere, from what I can tell. It's almost as if she's dropped off the grid."

"If I'd learned what she had about the Exodus seeds, I would too," I declare. "Still, she's going to surface for some reason. And it may be close by, since she's only been gone a couple of days."

Emma frowns. "Um…no. She left over a month ago."

"Are you saying Jilly wasn't his last file clerk?" I ask. "Odd. But Wellborne did mention two clerks before me. He said one had been there six months, and another just a little under a month."

"Then Jilly would have been the former," Emma assures me. "She quit over a month ago. From what the SeedPlenish employee roster shows, another woman—Serena Lee—was hired to replace her."

Jack shakes his head. "Jeez, I wonder what happened to her?"

"Emma, what can you pull up on this Serena person?" I ask.

"Let me see." She pulls an iPad from the stroller bag.

A moment later, she exclaims, "Bingo! I started with her SeedPlenish personnel file. Take a look at this!"

Her screen is open to Serena Lee's employee badge picture: Only it's Liang Xia.

"Well, I'll be damned," Jack declares.

"If she showed up the same time Jilly disappeared, maybe she had something to do with it," I declare.

"Obviously, Jilly was on to Wellborne's shenanigans," Jack reasons. "If Xia was his MSS contact, he may have called her in to clean up his mess."

"Sadly, you're right," Abu says. "And here's the proof."

We turn to find him standing in the doorway. He holds a picture in his hand. In it, a woman's head can be seen in a SeedPlenish seed bag. Her eyes are wide open. There is a bullet wound through her forehead. The bag is large enough to hold the rest of her.

"What a shame," I murmur. "Who is it?"

"She's the woman you replaced in Wellborne's office: Jilly McIntosh." There's an edge to Jack's voice.

I know what he's thinking: I might have met the same fate, if he hadn't gotten to Wellborne and me.

There's a good chance that he's right about that.

But who killed her: Wellborne or Xia? I guess we'll never know.

"The one link that will categorically tie Wellborne to MSS is the money that came into the Caymans bank account," Jack reminds us. "We should retrieve it."

"I've got operatives pulling Wellborne from the silo as we speak. We'll copy his prints. Once we get them, I'm sending Dominic to the Caymans to claim the funds and close it down." Ryan nods toward Jack and me. "In the meantime, you should hit the road for Dixon. And take some matches and butane. The sooner Exodus is annihilated, the better."

Crop Circles

Crop circles are large patterns created by people who think it's fun to flatten the stalks of a farm's crop, be it corn, oats, grass, or rapeseed.

Typically, these formations are quite intricate.

That being said, if you're a farmer whose livelihood depends on what you raise and sell, you may not exactly appreciate a bunch of drunken bozos wandering through your field and ruining your crops, let alone be awestruck at the beauty of their handiwork.

The paths they make zigging and zagging through your crops as you spray them with buckshot may not be half as pretty, but you'll certainly find it a lot more satisfying.

CLOVER HILL FARMS runs east along INTERSTATE 580, JUST

below the Northern California town of Dixon. Arnie has been able to access the SeedPlenish sales file on the farm's owners, Kerri and Kurt Clement. They not only purchase corn seed from SeedPlenish, but soy as well.

Like most of SeedPlenish's accounts, the Clements have enjoyed quantity discounts based on how much seed they order. However, one order in particular stands out like a sore thumb because the discount makes it a negligible purchase: it is listed on their billing account as EX-0001.

"For Exodus, perhaps?" Jack asks.

"We'll find out when we get there," I reason.

Also in the Clements' dossier is intel gathered from social media. The Clements' Facebook and Instagram accounts show their pride in their fifteen-hundred-acre farm, which Kurt's family has owned for five generations. In one photo, Kurt, jacked and blond, stands tall beside a row of corn, his arms crossed proudly at his chest. Another photo shows Kerri, slim-bodied but round-faced with strawberry-blond plaited pigtails, cradling a large watermelon under each arm. Both are in their mid-thirties.

They have no children. Their social media postings aren't personal, but specifically about the farm's prosperity: things like harvesting yields of their crops, or photos of their fields. In other words, their farm is not just their livelihood, but their life as well.

Acme's pilot, George Taylor, lands our helicopter in a meadow close to Clover Hill Farms' field of corn, but outside of the fence that surrounds the property. It's not yet sunrise, but there is a light on downstairs, in the kitchen of the two-story clapboard house beside the barn.

Jack and I make our way to the back door. His knock gets Kerri's attention. She stops her pot-scrubbing in order to dry her hands before coming to the door to see who's there at this ungodly hour.

When she gets to it, she doesn't open it, but stares out at us through the door's four-pane window. Her face is a mix of confusion and concern. "Can I help you?" she asks.

"Federal agents," Jack tells her. He holds up an official badge to prove it.

Perplexed, her eyes shift from his face to mine. She hesitates for a moment, then opens the door. "Why are you here? We only use documented workers on this farm, and we won't even hire for another month or so."

"Hasn't harvest started for you?" I ask.

She blinks twice before answering—a sure sign that what she's about to say won't necessarily be the truth. "Next week sometime."

"We're not here about undocumented workers," Jack explains. "Is Mr. Clement home? He'll also want to hear what we have to say."

"He's...ah, checking on something in one of the back fields. It's at least two miles down the road. I don't expect him back until lunchtime."

Again, the two blinks. I'd love to play poker with this woman. I'd clean up.

Jack raises a brow, so I know he catches it too. "Unfortunately, we have some bad news, and I'm sure he'll want to hear it. You see, we have reason to believe that a particular corn seed purchased by you—perhaps already planted for the upcoming harvest—includes a strain of toxins that are deadly for human consumption. It goes by the name of Exodus."

Hearing this, Kerri takes a step back. Her face loses all color. "But—you must be mistaken! I mean, sure, we were told that it's experimental, but Dr. Wellborne said that what makes it so wonderful, beyond its extraordinary yield capacity, is its ability to repel pests."

Perhaps pests have an innate ability to avoid plants that are toxic to them, but this is not something I need to share with Kerri Clement while she's having a meltdown.

"Dr. Wellborne talked to you directly about it, as opposed to your SeedPlenish sales rep?" Jack asks.

"Yes. I thought it was strange that he made the trip here, to the farm. But he told us that he wanted to personally invite us to be the test farm for Exodus, since we have an ideal growing situation. You see, we use only natural pesticides, but at the same time, we aren't opposed to using GMO strains. Dr. Wellborne also guaranteed that our full crop would be purchased upon harvest by a specific broker who distributes to a variety of food manufacturers. That way, SeedPlenish would get specific feedback regarding the end-use quality."

"So, you've received the check," I say, matter-of-factly.

"Um…no. Not yet." Again, two blinks.

Jack smiles, hoping to put her at ease. "I think I should find Mr. Clement and fill him in on the situation. Mrs. Stone will finish up with a few more questions. How can I reach him in the back field?"

"Follow the path by the house. At the fork, between the two corn fields, turn left, which will take you north. He's running the harvester, so he may not be able to hear you. You can use this flashlight to get his attention." She hands him one of several portable lights lined up on one of the kitchen's counters.

Jack nods in appreciation and heads out.

She waits until Jack leaves before turning to me. "What if we just return the seeds?"

"You can't. You've already planted them." I point to the acres of corn out the window, where the aqua-hued stalks catch the first rays of morning sun.

She frowns. She realizes that it's a gotcha moment. "But we'll get to keep the money, right? We didn't know they were tainted, and he promised us!"

"From what we know so far, Dr. Wellborne wasn't authorized by SeedPlenish to create the seed strain, let alone deliver it on the company's behalf. It may be an issue for the courts to sort out."

Her face turns to stone. "In the meantime, we lose our farm because we trusted SeedPlenish's top scientist that it was a sure thing? Why, you're—you're going to bankrupt us!"

I pat her arm. "I'm sorry. I truly hope it isn't the case. But I think you'd have a rock-solid case against SeedPlenish."

She throws off my hand.

I take the hint—time to change the subject. "Mrs.

Clement, what is the name of the broker who came for the corn?" I ask.

She shrugs. "I don't know off the top of my head." She points to the desk in the corner of the kitchen. "I'd have to look it up in Kurt's ledger."

She waits for my nod before heading to the desk.

What she pulls out isn't a ledger. It's a gun.

"Put your hands over your head," she commands.

"Kerri, you don't realize the importance of this. People's lives are at stake!"

"Including ours. If we lose the farm, we have nowhere else to go! Kurt will never get over it!"

"Just how do you think he'd feel knowing that he's responsible for the death of a staggering number of people? If that corn gets out, we're talking about a body count that could climb into the tens of thousands! The Exodus strain carries a deadly virus!"

She wavers, but only for a second. "It's already out—and…I…I can't be responsible for that! It wasn't our fault!"

"No one said it is. But we have to call the broker, to stop it from leaving his warehouse."

"How do you know he wasn't in cahoots with Dr. Wellborne?"

"I don't," I admit. "But if you let it go any further, you're just as guilty as anyone else who knows about it but does nothing to stop it."

"Kurt and I will be blamed anyway! Do you think anyone else will buy corn from us, once they hear about our role in this thing? And what about the seeds? Don't you know birds pick it up and move it—not to mention the wind? Our land will always be tainted. Hell, we won't even be able to sell the farm"—she pauses, as the full extent of her situation hits her—"unless—unless no one finds out where the seeds came from. So, just shut up"—she cocks the pistol —"or I'll do something you'll regret, because believe me, I have nothing to lose."

I do as I'm told—for now.

She frisks me for a gun and finds one in the holster strapped to my back. With her free hand, she hides it in a kitchen drawer, then reaches for the wall phone, where she presses autodial and hits the speaker button.

A man's voice exclaims, "Yep, what's up, hon?"

Kerri picks up the receiver so that I can't hear Kurt's responses to what she has to say. "We have visitors...*Feds*. They came to confiscate the crop....I know, Kurt! Calm down! Listen—I agree! One is coming your way. Don't worry, it's—*manageable*. Trust me! Don't...just do it—I don't know, an *accident*. I'm covering the other one, here. But be careful! He's got a gun...The drone? Great idea. You have it in the cab, right?" A look of relief sweeps over her face. "Kurt, I—I love you."

Touching, what we do for love.

She clicks off. She takes a step closer. "I'm sorry, but this is the end of the road for you."

"You're making a big mistake, Kerri. If you kill us, you'll have two murder convictions on your hands. Don't forget, California still has the death penalty."

"Sorry, but if we let you take our crop, we might as well

be dead—at least, as far as the bank is concerned! This farm has been in my husband's family for four generations. Sorry, but we'll take our chances that they'll never find your body out here—that is, if Kurt decides to bury you at all. The hogs in the barn will be glad to take care of the problem." With the pistol barrel, she nudges me toward the door. "Let's walk."

It's perhaps one hundred feet from the house to the barn. Next to it is the pigpen. Yes, I'd say the Clements' hogs would enjoy something other than the corn they're being fed.

Perhaps even more, considering all the vomit and diarrhea in the pen. I count twelve hogs. Two of them are laid out on their sides. Their eyes, open even in death, are covered in feasting flies.

Another four swine are also off their feet and wailing in pain.

I point at the pen. "Kerri, do you want to see the effect of the Exodus strain? Just look at what's happening to your hogs."

"Oh—my God!" She glances over quickly. When she sees what I see, she gasps and stares. "What the hell?"

I scoop down, grab a fistful of dirt, and fling it at her eyes.

"Shit!" she screams. It's a direct hit. She tries to wipe it away with her free hand, but at the same time she waves the gun in my direction and shoots wildly.

The bullet ricochets off a metal barrel, and into the pigpen. One of her pigs cries out with a death squeal.

She probably did it a favor.

Instinctively, Kerri's head turns toward the sound.

I tackle her so hard that she flips, head first, over the top rail of the pigpen.

Yuck.

She's laying there, arms and legs askew.

Her neck is broken. The pigs that are not yet ill feast on all the fresh meat in front of them. Sadly, Kerri is no exception.

I turn my head, but I still heave.

I'll never eat pork again.

When I can lift my head, I realize I have to warn Jack that he's walking into an ambush.

I run down the road as fast as I can.

DAMN IT, I FORGOT THAT KERRI TOOK MY GUN.

I stop short, and consider the possibility of heading back for it, but veto the notion. Even with a gun, Jack won't have the advantage of hiding if Kurt launches his drone.

I'll certainly add an element of surprise.

Then I hear it: the sound of a corn harvester. The big header in front can take down eight rows at once: chopping stalks and leaves, husking the ears, and pulverizing everything else in its wake. It's somewhere deep in the field beside me, but getting closer. I turn around—

I'm staring at it:

Like, say, right on my heels.

I feel an arm around my waist. In the nick of time, Jack pulls me out of the way.

I follow his lead, dodging through the corn. "Don't run down a row," he shouts. "Zigzag through the field—and stay out of the line of his turning radius, or you could get caught under one of the threshing wheels!"

"He's…he's tracking us with a drone," I gasp.

Jack looks up. "Okay, then we need to separate."

"You'll have to shoot it down. My gun is in the house, so I'll play decoy."

"Be careful! That machine cuts a wide berth."

I nod, then head left. He goes to the right.

I RUN OUT INTO THE ROAD.

The drone hovers in mid-air over the center of the field.

I shoot it a bird.

I must have caught its attention, because it veers my way.

We're off to the races.

The sound of a row of ten-foot-tall corn stalks crashing into one another, and yet another, is akin to what we all imagine a giant's footsteps would sound like. I don't have the advantage of height to see if I should run left or right in order to avoid getting shredded to death.

So, I just keep running.

Suddenly, I hear a dull buzzing coming from above. The next thing I know, something comes crashing down behind me.

Ding, dong, the drone is dead. Jack must have made a direct hit.

Like Cyclops, Kurt is now driving blind through the field. I hear the corn harvester turning in my direction, so I leap into a dense row of corn.

One of the corn harvester planter's fangs rips at my shirt. I groan at the pain from the gash in my arm, but I keep moving.

Kurt can't back it up, or else he may mangle the blades on his harvester. If he's going to follow me, he's going to have to take another wide turn. This gives me the break I need: to get behind the harvester, as opposed to in front of it.

I run alongside of it until I grab hold of the back ladder and leap onto it.

He feels my presence and turns around. He's shocked to see me there. He speeds up, hoping to shake me off. When he can't, his only alternative is to open the cab and grab hold of me.

He reaches for me, but I dodge his grip. He's mad enough to come at me again. But this time, when his head comes out of the cabin, despite the speed of the harvester, Jack is close enough to take his shot.

The bullet hits him in the chest. His body slams into the cab, only to bounce off, right into the harvester's blades.

As he's mangled, the machine grinds to a halt.

I reach into the cab to turn off the engine, but I'm not going to look at Kurt.

The sun has risen. The stalks look like a turquoise sea. On

any other day, in any other cornfield, this sight would be beautiful.

Kerri was right. The broker's name is in Kurt's ledger. It's Barnaby Phillips out of Bakersfield. He purchased seven acres of the stuff, the equivalent of eight hundred and forty bushels.

We hang tight until the FDA agents show up. Their directive is to confiscate enough of the corn to make the case, and to flash incinerate the rest, so that no residue is left.

I'm taking corn off the family menu, at least for now. I don't think I'll get an argument from Jack.

8

Spreading Manure

Despite the stench, organic matter excreted by animals is a nitrogen-rich soil amendment and fertilizer. Sometimes in the fall, farmers till green (that is, fresh) manure into the soil, giving its nutrients time to be released before the spring planting. Otherwise, it can "burn," or dehydrate them.

A more efficient way to spread manure is by first composting it for a time, with a carbon-rich bedding, such as hay, wood shavings, or straw. You'll know it's ready when it's a beautiful, crumbly, black, odor-free substance.

Should you be holding some bad guy hostage and interrogation is necessary, I'm sure that your methods will lead to the release of his own fresh manure. By all means, save it for your garden! Your roses and ranunculus will appreciate your thoughtfulness!

And should your prisoner expire during the course of your

interrogation, never fear: a decomposing body makes for a nutrient-rich fertilizer too!

ABU ALREADY HAS A TRUCK PULLED IN FRONT OF FARM FRESH Ventures when Jack and I get there. The produce brokerage, owned by Barnaby Phillips, is located outside Bakersfield, right off its principle highway, Route 99, not far from Interstate Highway 5. These two roads run the length of California's agriculturally rich central valley. We are parked in front of a warehouse surrounded by several silos of different sizes. Giant plastic blow-up corn is tethered on the warehouse's roof. The wind is brisk, making the loose green husks sway like a hula skirt, and its polyester corn silk shoot straight up over its head.

Polyester is the fabric of choice for Barnaby Phillips too. Considering his territory is all of California and Arizona, I'm surprised his suits don't melt into his skin. Thank goodness for cotton undershirts and tighty-whities.

Before we go inside, we call Ryan to discuss a strategy, since Jack and I are split on what will work best. "Should we level with the guy?" Jack asks.

"But, if we tell a civilian, it'll cause a panic," I counter. "Why not just buy the Exodus seeds outright?"

Ryan thinks about it for a moment. Finally, he says, "I agree with Donna. POTUS's mandate is that this mission be wrapped up without the public knowing there was even a possibility of an outbreak, let alone an outbreak because of an act of terrorism."

"Yeah, okay. So, what price do we offer him?"

"Give me a moment, so that I can look up the going rate for a bushel of corn…okay, it looks like it's around three dollars and eighty-four cents per bushel."

"The Clements' ledger showed only seven acres of the stuff was planted. It yielded an average of one-hundred and fifty bushels per acre," Jack points out.

Ryan pauses to calculate a dollar total. "That's four-thousand and thirty-two dollars."

"That was chump change for the Clements. No wonder they jumped at the opportunity for that extra million bucks Wellborne paid them to be the 'test farm' for the Exodus seed," I add. "By the way, Ryan, I don't think he'll take my Visa card."

"Very funny. When the time comes I'll do a direct deposit into his account."

Jack and I exchange looks. I'm sure he's thinking what I'm thinking: *If* the time comes.

It may not, if the corn has already been sold.

What a nightmare that will be.

BARNABY PHILLIPS SITS AT AN OLD METAL DESK IN THE MIDDLE of the warehouse's reception area. The twenty-by-ten paneled room doesn't hold much else, except for a couple of vertical file cabinets and a broken couch that sags against the far wall.

Barnaby is so busy good-ol'-boy-ing somebody on his desk phone that he doesn't hear us enter. Jack lands on the couch so hard that it groans as it rocks back onto its hind legs.

This certainly gets Barnaby's attention.

I elect to stand against the wall.

He holds up a finger, signaling us that he'll only be a moment longer.

By his chuckles and comments, he's being optimistic. "Yeah, boy, I hear ya…Yeah, boy, that was one whopper of a yield…the name of that waitress at Hot Wheels on Interstate 10? Wasn't it Jolene?" He chuckles. "Yeah…you can say *that* again."

Barnaby looks over at me, and gives me a wink.

How badly does he want to hold on to that eye?

When he sees that I'm not smiling, he shrugs. "What's that—the *Mustang Ranch*? Ha! You don't say! Well, in hindsight, I wouldn't doubt it. She could suck the chrome off of a—"

He doesn't get to finish his overused metaphor because I've slammed the phone receiver into its cradle.

He tries to hide his annoyance with a grin that shows a bumper crop of bad teeth. "So, now, what can I do for you folks?"

Jack smiles back. I have no issue with him playing good cop—for as long as *that* lasts. "We'd like to buy some corn. Specifically, the corn that came from Clover Hill Farms."

"Clover Hill?" Barnaby taps his forehead, as if the name escapes him.

"You know, the Clements' place." Jack's smile stays in place, but I notice he's balled his fists.

Barnaby must notice too, because he snaps his fingers as if his memory has suddenly come back to him. "Oh, yeah! Right! They grow some good ear up there in Dixon, don't they?" He leans back in his chair—unfortunately, too far, because it almost tips over. He rights himself quickly. "I've got it right out back." He motions to one of the silos outside the window.

"All one thousand and fifty bushels?" I ask.

Barnaby frowns. "You want it all?"

"Yes," Jack and I say in unison.

He looks at us suspiciously. "What kind of business do y'all have?"

"It's for…" *Hmmm.* Let me think fast. "A restaurant," I say at the same time Jack says, "Food processing."

Barnaby's head turns from Jack to me to Jack again.

"We process a lot of food in our restaurant," I explain. "People like to take home big to-go bags. So, we use up a lot of corn meal. We're now making our own meal, from scratch."

"Yeah…I get it." Barnaby shrugs. "You must sell a heck of a lot of corn dogs."

"The chef,"—I point to Jack—"is very particular about the ingredients. The Clements' corn comes highly recommended."

"So I hear." Barnaby lumbers over to the file cabinet,

comes up with whatever paperwork he needs, and sits back down. His knuckles roll across the calculator. "Okey-dokey, folkies! We're looking at five thousand five hundred bucks. Wanna pony up to the bar?" He looks up, expectantly.

Jack frowns as he cracks his knuckles. "Don't you mean three-thousand six hundred and forty eight dollars?"

Barnaby winces, but is smart enough to recalculate. I'd love to see what is really on his calculator tape. My guess is that the right figure is apt to come from a room full of chimpanzees diddling calculators before we ever get a straight answer from him.

"Why, what do you know?" he chortles. "You hit the number right on the head! We'll take a check, and you can come and pick it up in three days."

"We prefer to do direct deposit, and take it with us now." Jack points to Abu's truck.

Barnaby frowns. "Yeah, okay. Tell your driver to roll it under the number three silo, there."

Jack heads out the door, while Barnaby gives me the bank number for the deposit.

A few minutes later, the deposit is made. "Nice doing business with you," he hollers, as I run out the door.

Jack has already helped position the truck bed. He climbs up to the silo's funnel—the hopper. Abu and Jack are already wearing facemasks, eye goggles, and gloves. There are some in the truck for me as well. After we're done loading the corn, we'll meet FDA agents at a truck stop off I-5 to hand over the truck, and go home from there.

As I watch the corn fall out of the silo's hopper into the truck bed I think, All's well that ends well.

Or not.

Something is wrong: the color of the corn kernels. It isn't right.

I wave my hands to get Jack and Abu's attention. "This isn't the right corn! Look at the color. It's more yellow than orange."

They stare down at me, then into the truck bed. Jack slams the silo with his fist. "Damn it, you're right! Why, that son of a bitch!" He jumps off the silo ladder and runs toward Barnaby's office. "The son of a bitch is gone!"

I'm on the phone to Ryan. "Barnaby must be in on it. He gave us the wrong corn, and ran off, but he couldn't have gotten too far."

"Emma will text you his home address, his car's make and license, and any surveillance video we find on him during the past hour."

It doesn't take long before Emma calls back. "We lucked out! He's down at the bank branch where we wired the money. Go south on 99, until you get to Taft Highway, then make a right. You'll see it on the right side—the National Bank of Bakersfield."

"What's he driving?" Jack asks.

"A brand spanking new Ford F150 XLT. It still has the dealer's plates."

"Thanks, Emma," I say. "We're on it."

I shouldn't let Jack drive when he's so pissed. Suddenly, I feel sorry for Barnaby.

You should always look in the back seat of your car before you get in. You never know who'll be there, waiting for you, perhaps with a gun.

In Barnaby's case, it's Jack.

He waits until Barnaby tosses a briefcase filled with cash into the passenger seat and heaves himself into the driver's seat of his brand new Ford F150 XLT before sticking the barrel of his gun on the back of Barnaby's neck.

I open the passenger door, grab the briefcase, and hop in beside Barnaby. "I suppose you wanted to get this money so you could hand over our refund. Let's not play games, where's the corn?"

Barnaby is white around the gills, but he's still able to mutter, "It's…it's gone."

"Where?" Jack asks.

When Barnaby doesn't answer, he nudges the gun deeper into the base of his skull.

"Okay, okay! Just—don't shoot!" He takes a deep breath. "I have to look it up in my records."

"Slide over. She'll drive."

He doesn't argue, but he groans when I gun the engine before sliding his truck in front of a fast-moving van.

"Don't shit your pants, or there goes your new car smell," I warn him.

As it turns out, Barnaby waits until we're back at his office before he expels via a few choice bodily functions. I'm pretty sure that his pistol-whipping from Jack has something to do with it.

"Let's be clear. You say some of the corn went to the Farris Ranch feed lot, and to something called TasTee Cereals in Pasadena? And that the balance went to Disneyland, for the corn-on-the-cob booth in Frontierland?"

It's hard to talk when your mouth is stuffed with your own socks, but Barnaby was whimpering so loudly that it was a necessary evil.

The way he's hogtied, he's lucky Jack didn't cram a corncob into it, or any other orifice, for that matter.

It'll take the FDA agents another hour to get here. In the meantime, Abu stands guard while I've been rummaging through Barnaby's file cabinet for the paperwork that verifies his claims. "Is there anything you're leaving out?" I ask.

He shakes his head emphatically.

"Think hard," Jack warns him.

"Mmmm!" Barnaby exclaims. "FIWZ!"

I look over. "It sounds as if he said 'Fiwz.'"

Jack shrugs. "Maybe he likes the taste of his own socks."

Barnaby shakes his head again, but even harder this time. "Naaah! Fiwz Cowa—"

"Jack, he's choking. Do something."

Jack sighs, but pulls out the sock anyway.

It takes a moment for Barnaby to catch his breath. "Fizz All-Natural Cola! Santa Ana!"

"What does a cola company need with corn?" Jack wonders out loud.

Barnaby shrugs. "Fizz makes its own corn syrup from scratch. That way, it can claim it only uses all natural ingredients. "

"There's nothing 'all natural' about GMOs," Jack snorts. "Why wouldn't it use cane sugar instead?"

"Sucrose is sucrose," I point out. "And corn syrup is certainly cheaper than cane sugar." I move to the next file drawer and rummage through it. "Found it." I wave the contract triumphantly.

Jack kneels down, so that he's face-to-face with Barnaby. "How much did Wellborne pay you to distribute the corn?"

"A…mill—above my broker's fee, of course."

Jack nods. "Well, sure, of course."

He crams the sock back into Barnaby's mouth.

Barnaby moans deliriously as we walk out the door.

FARRIS RANCH IS THE LARGEST FEEDLOT IN THE WEST. LAST year, Jeff did a report on it for his California history class. "Did you know over one-hundred and fifty million pounds of beef moves through Farris Ranch in a single year?" Jeff proclaimed to the family. "Over one-hundred-thousand head of cattle live on a thousand acres. They harvest hundreds of them each day."

"They don't 'live' there. They *die* there," Mary pointed

out. "When you say, 'move through' and 'harvest,' you do know those terms mean 'slaughter,' don't you?"

"They kill cows at the stinky place?" Trisha asked. We've driven by it enough times that its signature scent—manure and urine—is indelibly embedded in her young mind. She looked down at the burger on her dinner plate. The tears fell fast and furious as she ran from the table.

She vowed never to eat hamburgers, ever again.

That lasted about a month. How soon we forget.

By helicopter, Farris Ranch is only a half-hour south, down I-5. As always, there is a constant flow of traffic heading to and from the state's largest metropolitan areas, Los Angeles and San Francisco, Oakland, and San Jose.

Until we're a mile from the ranch.

Below us, cars are skidding to avoid a fourteen-car pile-up, and the cause of it: a stampede of cattle that has crossed the northbound expressway lanes. As they rampage through the center median and into southbound traffic, a Land Rover veers right to avoid the herd, only to collide with a tractor-trailer truck. The force sends the smaller vehicle flying—

Into the oncoming cattle.

It takes out the lead steers. The big rig rolls forward into the rest.

The whole herd disappears behind a curtain of dust.

From our height and with the thumping of the helicopter blades, I can only imagine the sound of screeching tires and crunched metal, not to mention the cries coming from the wreckage.

Eight cars skid into the mess, like bumper cars at a county fair.

The only good news: none of the herd survives.

GEORGE LANDS THE COPTER IN A MEADOW NEAR THE FEEDLOT. Jack and I run through the hole in the fence and through flattened manure created by the stampede, toward the long, endless rows of feed bunks.

Those cattle that haven't stampeded are chomping on the tainted corn.

Others angrily rampage through the lot, slamming into other cows.

That is, the ones still standing.

"It's like mad cow disease," Jack shouts at me. "Donna, we have to cover these feed bunks."

I follow his lead, shutting the gates that allow the cows to access the feed bunks. When the cows realize our game plan, they get huffy. One butts Jack's back with his head. Another rams the gate beside me. I leap out of the way just in time.

That's when we see the men—three of them, face down in the sludge.

From the looks of things, they were killed in the stampede. We kneel beside each one, placing two fingers on their necks hoping to find a pulse and not surprised when we don't.

We look around us. What we see is scary. It's as if the whole herd is watching our every move.

"It's like that Hitchcock movie, *The Birds*, only it's —*cows*," I murmur.

Especially when the whole herd begins to move in our direction at once.

Over the snorts of angry cows headed our way, I can barely hear Jack shout, "Let's get out of here!"

We don't have much of a head start. Worse yet, the faster we run, the more cattle fall in behind the lead steer.

Jack grabs my hand and starts running toward the slaughterhouse and ranch office. We crest the hill—

To find a war zone in front of us. Fire leaps from the roof of the slaughterhouse. The sound of cattle mooing frantically fills the air. Trampled human bodies are all over the parking lot.

But we can't turn around. The stampeding herd is just fifty yards away.

Jack slams into me. We fall to the ground.

No, into a culvert.

Just in time too. It's deep enough that the cattle fly over, only to lose their balance and tumble down the hill. Some land hard, breaking their front legs. Those following fall on top of the lead steers.

Jack is draped over me. I close my eyes, and cover my ears. I pull my shirt up to cover my nose and mouth hoping to save myself from the dust and dirt. I lose my sense of place with the thunderous pounding and grunting of these beasts rushing past me. I only know I'm somewhere deep within this haze of dust swirling above us.

Suddenly, like a tornado, it vanishes as quickly as it

appeared. I open my eyes to see that Jack's are still closed. His face—all of him—is caked in dust. I'm sure I am too.

At least we're still alive.

He rises slowly. Whatever he's looking at has him shaking his head in wonder. Finally, he takes my hand and pulls me to my feet. "Ryan needs to know, so that this can be contained as soon as possible. Let's get out of here. No sudden moves. If one comes after us, shoot to kill."

He doesn't have to tell me twice.

We make our way back through that same spot where the fence had been torn open, and return to our helicopter.

Thankfully, George had already called Ryan with a heads-up on what was happening on the highway, so the call to Ryan is quick and dirty.

"A HazMat battalion is on its way," he barks. "Donna, POTUS needs to be briefed as soon as possible."

In other words, put in a call.

Lee isn't going to like what I have to tell him. I try his number.

It immediately rolls over into voice mail. "We've had a development."

George starts the engine. He doesn't ask questions. Even if he had, we'd have a hard time explaining what we just saw:

Cowmageddon.

9

Germination

The process that transports the embryo within a seed into its next step—sprouting into a seedling—is called germination. Seed germination depends on both internal and external factors. Internally, all fully developed seeds contain embryos, as well as a place to store food reserves, usually wrapped in a seed coat. Externally, germination is affected by such factors as oxygen, water, light, and temperature.

This is not the same as the process of germaphobia in humans, which usually takes place when one comes in contact with something that makes one ill. However, there are ways to live germ-free. For example, you can:

1. *Carry a surgical mask. True, you'll look silly and paranoid. To deflect pitying glances, wear surgical scrubs too. That way, you can claim, "The operation was a success." Or:*

2. *Carry hand sanitizer. Most come as scented gels, foams or liquids that can be applied right on the fingers and palms. Note of caution: whereas the base of most hand sanitizers is alcohol, resist the urge to guzzle the stuff. This type of alcohol—isopropyl—will do worse than give you a hangover. It'll be the death of you.*

"WHAT'S FOR DINNER?" JEFF ASKS. UP UNTIL NOW, HE'S BEEN shooting hoops in the driveway with Morton and Cheever.

"Eggplant lasagna," I declare. As proof, I hold up the eggplant slices in my hands, which I've been scattering over layers of noodles and ricotta cheese.

Jeff heads back out the kitchen door to yell, *"It's eggplant lasagna!"*

Even from where I'm standing, I hear Cheever gagging.

I guess we won't be having dinner guests. Fine by me.

Trisha wrinkles her nose. "I'm glad I'm eating out."

I turn to my youngest. "Whoa, whoa! Says who?"

"Janie's in town. Aunt Phyllis said it was okay!"

"Did…did Janie's mother call to invite you?"

"No. It was somebody called an aide." Trisha wrinkles up her nose. "Mommy, what's an aide?"

Mary looks up from her *Vogue* magazine. "It's a person whose job is to help someone more important."

"Janie isn't important. Why would she have an aide?"

"Maybe it's her mother's aide," I explain. "Or…her father's." Is Lee in town too? That would be convenient—

For him and Acme, if not for me.

"I'm eating out tonight too. Everyone was invited to sleep over at Sara's. I cleared it with Aunt Phyllis." Mary folds her arms at her waist, as if bracing for a fight.

Yes, she'll certainly get one from me. "By 'everyone,' I presume you mean Tara and Cara too?" I know trouble when I smell it. This stinks as badly as Farris Ranch. "Earth to Aunt Phyllis!" I shout loud enough for my aunt to hear me in the great room. She's enthralled in a rerun of *Antiques Roadshow.*

When she doesn't respond, I walk over and click off the television with the remote.

Phyllis practically leaps off the couch. "Why did you do that? Leigh Keno was going to tell that woman how much that piece of crap table of hers is worth!"

"More importantly, why would you allow the girls to go to sleepovers? Have you forgotten that it's a school night, and they have homework?"

"No, I didn't forget," Aunt Phyllis sniffs. "Girls, who's finished her homework?"

Mary and Trisha raise their hands.

Aunt Phyllis points to the girls. "Satisfied?"

"No, not really." I turn to Mary. "I'd like to speak with Sara's mother, to make sure she's onboard with this."

"Sure, okay," Mary says uncertainly. She picks up her cell phone and punches just one digit. To my chagrin, Sara has earned an autodial.

"Sara, hi! Um…listen, my mom wants to check with your mom, to see if sleeping over tonight is okay…Oh! Sure,

I'll put her on." Mary thrusts the phone practically in my face.

"Hello, this is Brenda Lowell. And you are?" Now I know where Sara gets her imperious manner.

"I'm Mary's mother, Donna. I want to confirm that my daughter sleeping over tonight will in no way inconvenience you."

"Not at all." I shiver at the frost in her voice. "If you don't mind, I have to ring off. I was making hamburger patties for the girls. The others are already here."

Yuck.

I bite my lip before asking her where it came from. If what Ryan says is true—that for what we know, no beef left Farris Ranch—they're in the clear. "I'll drop her off in half an hour. Thanks ag—" She hangs up before I can finish my sentence.

The nut doesn't fall far from the other nut.

I look down at my eggplant. So much for a healthy meal with the whole family.

That's okay. It should be ready by the time Jack gets home with Evan from lacrosse practice. Jack is at Acme, briefing Ryan on the Exodus situation.

I turn to the girls. "Grab your overnight gear. I'll take you as soon as I've put the lasagna in the oven. Aunt Phyllis, will you listen for the timer?"

She waves from the couch. Leigh and his twin, Leslie, are one-upping each other on the historical significance of a Louis XIV side chair owned by a clueless retiree in Sarasota.

Yeah, okay, we'll see if she's paying attention.

I hope I don't come home to a four-alarm fire.

I PULL UP TO SARA'S HOUSE FIRST. SHE LIVES IN THE FAR END OF Hilldale, in a three-story Mediterranean stucco, fronted by a velvety lawn dotted with birches, and edged by a box hedge. The driveway juts out to accommodate a half-court basketball hoop, where Sara, Cara, and Tara are taking turns doing jump shots.

Before Mary hops out of the car, she turns to me, "Would you care to come in and meet Sara's mom?"

I force a smile on my lips as I consider her proposal. The advantage of saying yes is that I might get over my qualms that I'm leaving my daughter with a coven of bitches. On the other hand, I already don't like the woman, and I'd hate for Mary to see the evidence of that on my face. I don't need her being even more defensive of Sara. "No, it's not necessary. Please thank her again for me."

"Mom"—Mary hesitates as she searches for her words —"I know Sara and the others can be a little…catty—even with me. But I'm part of the team now. We've all got to trust each other, both on and off the court."

I take hold of her hand. "No matter where you are in life, no matter who it is, trust has to be earned. Please, Mary, never forget that."

I've learned this lesson the hard way, and I'll do anything to keep my children from making the same mistake.

Mary frowns, but she nods nonetheless. She kisses me before bounding out of the car.

The girls run up to her for a group hug.

Sara catches my eye and waves goodbye.

There is nothing I can do but wave back.

Next up for the Stone shuttle service: Dropping Trisha at Lion's Lair, Hilldale's most palatial estate, which the fourth estate has dubbed, "the Western White House." I guess I shouldn't complain, since that distinction by the media has doubled home prices in Hilldale.

"You remember what we'll be doing this weekend, right?" Trisha asks.

I hate to tell her that I may be visiting a killer in a minimum-security prison. Instead, I say, "Working on your plant project?"

"Yes, but what else?" she prods gently.

"Okay, I give up."

Trisha sighs heavily at my memory loss. "Deliver Daisy Scout cookies!" At the thought, she hops up and down in her seat. "I've already made up a list of all our friends and family who ordered some. And Aunt Phyllis has already promised that if we have any boxes left over, she'll take me with her to Bingo one night next week, so that we can buttonhole all the people there." She frowns. "Mommy, what does 'buttonhole' mean?"

"It means to ask, hopefully as politely as possible."

"Oh!" Trisha nods as this sinks in. "So, it's not the same thing as 'strong-arm'?"

It's my turn to sigh. "That depends on who's doing it. If it's your Aunt Phyllis, more than likely, it's the same thing. However, if it's you or me"—I tweak her nose—"it's better that we buttonhole, because strong-arming really means forcing someone to do something that they may not want to do."

"In other words, it's not nice." She gives me the high sign. "Don't worry, Mommy. I'll always ask politely."

A moment later, we pull up at Lion's Lair. The estate has always had an impressive gate. Since Lee became president, a guardhouse has been added. I pull out my driver's license. A uniformed officer checks a manifest and waves us through.

We drive to the front rotunda to find Janie waiting outside to greet us—

With Lee.

Be careful what you wish for…

Janie runs to the passenger side of the car, where Trisha sits, but Lee is sauntering my way.

Trisha smacks a kiss on my cheek before grabbing her overnight bag and flying out the door. The girls hug each other so hard that it almost brings tears to my eyes, so I glance away.

When I look back over, Trisha catches my eye and waves. She watches curiously as Lee leans down so that we're eye level.

"A pleasure to see you again, Mrs. Stone," he says.

"And you, Mr. President. So glad you and the family have made it home for a few days."

"This time around, it's just Janie and me. Babette chose to stay in D.C. She's hosting a few Middle Eastern dignitaries."

"Sorry to have missed her." *Not.*

As if reading my mind, he laughs raucously. Curious, Trisha looks over, at us. I wave to her, as if saying, *Everything is fine.*

Not.

Janie, who is describing the new dress she'll be wearing to an upcoming state dinner, is oblivious to the look in her stepfather's eye when he smiles down at me. Trisha sees it, however. It puts a frown on her face.

"Do you have a few minutes for a chat?" Lee asks.

"I wish I could but I was in the middle of putting dinner on the table."

"I'm sure Jack won't mind if you take a few moments to update me on what you've been up to lately. Isn't that why you called me? I insist you stay for dinner too."

He's got me there. I purse my lips to keep from frowning. "Um…sure. I'll have to text Aunt Phyllis to remind her to pull out the lasagna, and to serve dinner without me. I turn off the car engine. I'd hoped to deliver the bad news about the Exodus seeds by phone instead. Oh well.

I know I should call Jack too, but I'd rather just explain when I get home.

Yes, okay, I'll admit it: *I'm a coward.*

"No problem," Lee says. "Take your time."

He watches as I tap out the message, then he opens the car door for me and takes my hand to help me out.

He keeps his hand on the small of my back as we move toward the home's grand entrance.

His move is noticed by Trisha. I can tell she doesn't like what she sees because she scowls.

When we're inside the grand foyer, he turns to Janie. "You girls can go and play. Mrs. Stone and I will be in the library until dinner is served."

Trisha tugs my hand. I bend down so that she can whisper in my ear: "Mommy, don't let him strong-arm you."

If only she knew.

LEE AND I ARE NOT ALONE AFTER ALL.

In fact, we're on a conference call. Lee begins, "Donna Stone, I'd like to introduce you to Secretary of Agriculture Harkness."

"A pleasure," a gruff voice mutters via Lee's speaker-phone. Lee must also note the obvious tension in the man's voice, because he grimaces.

"And, of course, your superior, Ryan Clancy, is also on the line."

"Donna, good of you to join us." I note the surprise in Ryan's voice.

"And Ryan tells me your mission leader, Jack Craig, is there in the office with him." Lee grins at me, as if to say, *Gotcha.* "Good evening, Jack."

"Hello, Mr. President," Jack's voice is civil. After a pause, he adds, "And Donna."

Not so civil.

Oh, well. As far as Jack is concerned, I don't have hope for the rest of the conversation, let alone the rest of the night.

Lee motions me to the couch. I presumed he'd take one of the wingback chairs flanking it, but I'm wrong. He waits until I lower myself onto it before sitting beside me.

When he reaches over to reposition the speakerphone, our knees touch. He doesn't pull away.

"I read Ryan's report on the containment of the Exodus seeds to date," Lee begins. "From what I understand from Secretary Harkness, both the SeedPlenish supply, and the Clements' fields, have been razed and tilled, and all silos have been emptied of their earlage."

"Another bit of good news," Ryan says. "One of our operatives, Dominic Fleming has retrieved the funds placed in Wellborne's Cayman Islands bank account. Our tech team is now tracing the funds' sender. We should know more about that in a couple of days."

"Oh?" Lee frowns. "I thought Acme already had intel in its possession that shows MSS's role in activating Exodus."

"It does," Jack says evenly. "But further verification, through a funds trace, gives your administration a major bargaining chip, should—God forbid—the press ever get ahold of this story. This should also be the irrefutable proof the Secretary of State may need to show his Chinese counterpart, in light of concessions that will need to be made."

"Frankly, I think the trace is a waste of Acme's time," Harkness growls.

"Let me be the judge of that," Lee barks back. He thinks for a moment. Finally, he adds, "Sure, do it. Ryan, report back to me with your results."

"Jack is running with it, Mr. President. He'll be happy to follow up—"

Lee interrupts, "That's okay. I'm sure Donna can keep me abreast, since she's doing so already."

Awkward silence.

Lee glances over at me.

If he's expecting a smile for getting me in Dutch with Jack, he's whistling *Dixie* in a Nor'easter.

"FDA investigators are interrogating SeedPlenish's executive staff in regard to both data and containment," Harkness pipes up. "Any word of this getting out will send SeedPlenish's stock plummeting, so it's in everyone's interest to cooperate."

"I know SeedPlenish's chairman personally," Lee says. "I'd be shocked if it went any higher than Wellborne."

"Yes, I'm sure it would be nice to clear one of your largest campaign contributors of any wrongdoing," Jack says dryly. "All the more reason to do a back-end investigation through SeedPlenish's financials, sales receipts or other connections they have with Chinese companies," Jack assures him. "If something comes up, you'll be the first to know."

"As for the Clements, not only was their livestock cremated, but—well, to be honest, they were too," Harkness continues.

Scary. But then again, so is the alternative. What if they had lived, and gotten away with this act of terrorism?

Still, I have to ask: "How will it be explained to their next-of-kin?"

Harkness' guffaw resonates through the room. "We're lucky that they had none. As for their farm, a third party is purchasing the property at auction. The ground will be dug up five feet deep, eliminating the chance for heirloom seeds to take root."

"And what about Barnaby Phillips?" Jack asks.

"Mr. Phillips is singing like a catbird," Harkness assures him. "He confirms that he was approached by Dr. Wellborne to work as the broker for the good doctor's test farm, and that he was paid a very generous bonus above his commission to do so."

"Which brings us to Farris Ranch," says Jack. "Our associate, Abu Nagashahi, confirms that the corn only arrived the night before the stampede. Since our arrival for containment, the FDA has confiscated all the corn on the premises, as well as all the cattle carcasses in the slaughterhouse. Abu also witnessed the extermination of all of the cattle in the feed lot." He sighs. "However, records at Farris Ranch show that two carcasses—calves, which fed on the corn—were purchased the same day of the stampede, by a private butcher based in Beverly Hills. Donna, you and I are checking into that situation tonight."

Ironically, I now have my excuse to pass on dinner with Lee.

"And there's still the corn heading to Fizz Cola in Santa

Ana, as well as TasTee Cereals, in Pasadena—not to mention Disneyland," Jack continues.

"This is turning into a nightmare," Lee murmurs, just loud enough for me to hear him. He closes his eyes. His head falls back against the couch.

Suddenly, I feel sorry for him. If Acme can't contain it, the whole world will blame him for what has transpired.

Truly, in all things political, the buck stops with Lee Chiffray.

I should resist the urge to pat his hand, but I don't.

He takes my hand in his, and squeezes it.

A shiver runs through me. He must feel it too, because he opens his eyes. His attempt at a smile is weak.

And yet, he doesn't let go.

"Gentlemen—and Mrs. Stone—thank you for your time and insights on this matter. Secretary Harkness, I appreciate your oversight. Ryan, as always, you've put together a stellar team. And Jack"—he hesitates—"this is one task in which I don't envy you."

This truly is leaving a lot unsaid: *In what way does he envy Jack?*

I'm not sticking around to find out.

I take my hand out from under his, and stand up.

He stands up too.

But before I can say anything, let alone walk to the door, he kisses me—

On the cheek.

His lips linger, but only for a second. Finally he says, "Stay safe. And by the way, you have a rain check—for tomorrow night. Jack can tag along, if he can stomach eating across from me."

I nod silently, then hurry out the door. I'm too shocked to say anything.

I come home to find Jeff, Evan, and Aunt Phyllis watching an episode of *House of Cards*. They chortle at the Macbethian antics of Frank Underwood and his wife, Claire.

I'm sure Jack will be back any time now. I should go upstairs and prepare for whatever awaits us. Instead, I stand at the doorway, watching them enjoy social commentary as dark farce.

Or is it?

Sometimes, I wonder if I'm a pawn in the real game of politics.

Finally, they notice me standing behind them. "All homework done?" I ask half-heartedly.

I only ask them because I know it's expected of me. Really, I want to shout, *Don't trust anyone! Take cover! Run for the hills! Hide!*

But seriously, what good will that do?

It won't. No one would believe what I have to say. It's like all those posts we see on activist blogs spouting conspiracy theories. The Kardashians are all anyone cares about.

Forget your troubles. Come on, get happy…

As if.

The boys give grudging waves followed by annoyed nods. Not that I blame them. They are good boys. They know it, and I know it too.

I'm truly blessed in so many ways.

"I have to go out." My pronouncement doesn't even earn me a raised eyebrow. "Brush your teeth before bedtime," I say, again, because it's expected of me.

And then, it strikes me that I haven't given Jeff a chance to shine and at the same time make myself happy—or to at least bring a little normalcy into my life. "Jeff, I forgot to ask: how did you do with your Social Studies paper?"

He purses his lips. Finally, he says, "He hasn't graded them yet. We get them back next week some time."

My son is lying to me.

And that, dear reader, is the icing on the cake of my day.

I can't deal with it now, so I run upstairs to get ready for Jack's inevitable call to arms.

10

Leaching

Leaching is the process in which excess salts or nutrients are removed from your garden's soil.

Sometimes, this is a good thing. For example, should you determine that your plants have been over-fertilized, you can use large quantities of fresh water to "wash" the soil.

It can also be a bad thing. In areas of extremely high rainfall, sometimes natural leaching takes place. In this case, in order for plants to thrive, an abundance of nutrients have to be introduced to the soil.

Leaching can take place in humans too. In Medieval times, it was presumed that leeches—used for the purpose of bloodsucking—could save one from a fatal illness by freeing your body of tainted blood.

This particular theory has been disproven.

That being said, however, putting a few of those leeches to work on those annoying busybodies who (metaphorically speaking) suck the life out of you may provide you with exactly what you need: nutrient-rich corpses that can help your garden grow.

"HOW'S LEE?" JACK ASKS, OH SO CASUALLY, WHILE WE'RE ON the 405, heading into Beverly Hills.

"As you might expect—worried that this whole thing might blow up in his face."

He shrugs. "You're just saying that to make me happy."

"No, I'm not. I'm saying it because it's true." Okay, now to prove that the best defense is a good offense. "I told you before the mission started that I was happy to let you keep Lee up to speed. If you—or for that matter, Ryan—changed your mind, you could have at least told me."

"Ryan set up the call to Lee, and told me about it just as I walked in. His next call was to be to you." He shakes his head angrily. "But, apparently, you already knew about the call, or you wouldn't have been there with Lee in the first place."

"Wrong again," I retort. "Janie invited Trisha for a sleepover. I was dropping my daughter off when the president came out to invite me in on the call."

"Oh? I thought he invited you in *for dinner.* At least, according to Aunt Phyllis." He turns toward me just in time to see my face go bright red.

"I...I couldn't say no, how could I?" I look out my side window. "I mean, would you have said no?"

"Probably not," he conceded. "But, then again, Lee has never asked me to dine with him." He pulls up in front of the butcher shop and stops the car.

"You're wrong," I declare blithely. "We're invited to dinner tomorrow night. Perhaps I should bow out, so that you two can come to some kind of understanding as to your roles in my life."

"That's for you to say," Jack says quietly. "Not him—or me. That is, unless you say yes to my umpteenth proposal of marriage. So, what do you say?"

Oh, brother. "Really, Jack Craig? You're asking me *now*?"

"I'm just trying to catch you between flirtations. Between missions, near-death experiences. Or between, quite literally, catching you."

"Why don't you try quote-unquote catching me when it's just the two of us, enjoying each other's company without a care in the world? Maybe you'll get the answer you want!" I jump out of the car, slamming the door after me.

This guy better not give us any grief. Seriously, I'm not in the mood.

It's after hours at the Beverly Hills Meat Market, but there's a light on in the rear of the building.

We walk around to that side. Through the frosted transom of the back door, I can make out a shadow of someone swinging something: a cleaver. It's a one-man operation and the owner's name is Jimmy Pennypacker, so that must be him.

"I guess we got here just in time," Jack murmurs. He raps on the door.

The figure's arm is raised. He freezes when he hears the knock. For the longest time, he does nothing. Finally, the cleaver rattles onto the table as he shuffles toward the door, but he doesn't open it. "Who the hell is it?" he growls.

"Federal agents, Mr. Pennypacker," Jack responds. "May we come in?"

"Not until you show me some ID." The man's tone is belligerent.

Jack holds up his badge.

Eventually, the man unlocks the door, but he stands in the threshold, making it hard for us to look past him.

He's big, brawny, and bucktoothed. The bib apron wrapped around his wide girth used to be white, but now it's so coated with blood that it's almost black.

"What's this about?" he mutters.

"Mr. Pennypacker, you purchased some beef this morning, from Farris Ranch. Unfortunately, it's tainted. We've come to retrieve it."

"It hasn't yet been distributed to customers, has it?" I ask.

For a second, Pennypacker's mouth hardens into a snarl. But, just as quickly, it curls back into a bucktoothed grin.

He shrugs. "It's on the table now, for a dinner tomorrow night. So, who's going to reimburse me for it?"

Jack hands him a card of one of the FDA agents. "You can take it up with him."

"Sure, whatever." He stands aside. Sweeping his hand through the air, he murmurs, *"Entrez vous."*

There's a chill in the air, and it's not just the air-conditioning.

"THAT'S ONE OF THEM, THERE ON THE COUNTER." HE POINTS TO the carcass he was cutting when we knocked on his door. It's small, so definitely that of a calf.

Jack opens the duffel and takes out two of everything: HazMat jumpsuits, pairs of gloves, facemasks, goggles, booties, and large zip-up body bags. Pennypacker leans up against the wall, as if watching us putting on these duds is part of some sleazy floorshow.

I say sleazy because he's practically salivating when I wiggle into my jumpsuit. "Need help with that zipper?" he offers with a leer.

"Thanks, but no thanks." Does he notice that I shudder? Yes. Does he give a damn? No. Instead, he giggles.

A big man with a girlish squeal and a bloody apron. Something tells me he doesn't date much.

Jack breaks the mood by asking, "Where's the second one?"

Pennypacker points to the walk-in refrigerator. "In there. Hook Eight."

"Donna, grab that one, will you? While I take this one out to the van."

I nod, take the second bag, and head toward the

refrigerator.

The door is made of heavy frosted glass. I open it, aligning the knob to a hook that allows it to stay open until I can drag out the carcass.

The refrigerator is cold and large. It's really two rooms, not one, because it angles around a corner. All the meat hooks have numbers scrawled above them. Besides the carcasses, it holds a rolling table.

I unzip the body bag, leaving it that way on top of the table. Next, I push the table until I'm in front of Number Eight. It is the last one on the left-hand side, before turning the corner.

I have to angle the carcass up a few inches before heaving it onto the table. It's heavy enough that when it lands, the table slides around the corner—

When I turn the corner to retrieve the cart, I discover the body of a naked young woman hanging from one of the hooks. Her lips are frosted, and her eyes are open.

"Ooops! You weren't supposed to see that," Pennypacker hisses behind me.

I turn to find him standing not ten feet away. He holds a cleaver in his hand.

I shove the rolling cart at him as hard as I can. The calf carcass gives it extra momentum. He grunts as it hits him square in the gut. It hurts enough that he's still bent over when he pushes it away, but it doesn't stop him from hurling his cleaver at me.

I duck just in time, and it pinwheels over me, creasing the wall just a few inches over my head.

I reach for it, but it's stuck firmly in the redwood paneling.

"I don't have time for this crap," he mutters. He yanks an empty hook off the wall.

Great idea. I do the same.

He's smart enough to keep the table between us. We circle each other like sumo wrestlers, looking for the perfect hold. His reach is longer than mine, so when he swipes his hook at me, I have to move fast.

Unfortunately, every time I take a step back, he moves the table even closer until I'm cornered against the wall, at which point he shoves the table away. "Sorry, bitch, but you and Muscles can't take the meat. It's got a date with destiny."

"I'll bet you say that to all the girls," I say. "By the way, is it working for ya?"

My sass puts him over the top. He charges me with his hook.

I grab hold of the two directly over my head, so that I'm hanging on them. Quickly, I bend my knees, raise my legs, and with all my might, I kick as hard as I can—

Catching him in the chest.

I've shoved him so hard that he smacks into the rolling table. It breaks his momentum and throws him off balance. It doesn't help that the bloody sawdust beneath his feet has him slipping and sliding backward across the floor, like a skater who has lost his balance while attempting a C-Cut. His hands twirl like pinwheels, but he can't stop his fall, slamming his head into the hard concrete floor.

At one point, he must have let go of the hook because it flies high over his head—

And ricochets off the ceiling—

Directly into his right eye.

I guess it doesn't matter, because I think he's already dead.

I ease myself down off the hooks and walk over. Had it not been for the sawdust soaking up the blood from the crack in his head, he'd be sporting a perfect halo of deep-red blood.

Jack sticks his head through the door. Seeing Pennypacker on the floor, he says, "Uh-oh."

"Frankly, I don't think he'll be missed. At least, not by her." I jab a thumb at the woman hanging on the wall.

Jack walks over to the dead woman. Staring up at her, he murmurs, "I wonder what his relationship, if any, was with her?"

"This guy was behaving weirdly from the moment we walked through the door. Her body might be a big part of the reason."

He shakes his head. "Let's grab the tainted carcass and get the hell out."

"But there's more to this than a dead body, Jack. Pennypacker said that the Exodus carcasses 'have a date with destiny.' Why would this guy want to hold on to tainted meat?"

"Good question." Jack walks out of the refrigerator, toward the desk. He rummages in the drawers until he finds what he's looking for: a delivery slip.

Attached to it is a check stub. The check is made out to cash, in the amount of one hundred thousand dollars. It is drawn from the same Cayman Islands bank we found in Wellborne's computer.

I look at the delivery address. "Oh, my goodness! It's supposed to be delivered to POTUS's house—for the dinner party he's throwing tomorrow night!"

Jack laughs. "If you want it, you now have the best excuse in the world to skip dinner at Lee's place again."

I sigh loudly. "You keep forgetting that you were also invited, remember?"

"Yes, but I had planned to pass on the honor. You know what they say: three's a crowd." He shrugs. "Should you ever say yes to my proposal, it'll be interesting to see if Lee will finally quit trying to seduce you. I guess we'll never find out."

"Oh? Why not?"

"Because you keep finding excuses to say no to me."

He doesn't wait for me to explain anything, let alone what will turn my no into a yes. Instead, he hands me the paperwork, then zips up the second carcass, throws it over his shoulder, and heads out the door.

On the drive home, I call Ryan to brief him on our run-in with the Butcher of Beverly Hills.

"I have a contact at Beverly Hills P.D.," Ryan says. "I'll give them a heads-up on what to expect."

My next call is to Lee, to explain how close he came to serving the tainted meat. "I'm sure you won't mind if Jack and I pass on dinner tomorrow. We'll take a rain check for when you and Babette are next in town."

"Sorry to hear that, but I guess I don't blame you. How do I break it to my constituents that I've gone vegan?" he says. From his tone, I don't think he's joking.

Jack heard me cancel for both of us, and yet, he says nothing.

That's okay. He's smiling.

It's late enough that by the time we get home from delivering the carcasses to Acme, Aunt Phyllis, Jeff, and Evan have already gone to bed.

At least, I presume so. I've just crawled into my side of the bed when my phone buzzes. It's our home security app, alerting me that the back door has opened.

A break-in is worthy of détente with Jack. I nudge him. When he rolls over, I hold my index finger against my mouth so that he doesn't make a sound when he sees what's on my cell phone screen: two figures can barely be made out, inching through the kitchen to the great room.

He nods, and rolls out of his side of the bed, crouching down so that he can pull his gun from under the vault concealed within the mahogany bed frame. I do the same on my side.

Silently, we open the bedroom door.

The intruders are taking the steps, one by one—

Until they hit the one step that creaks. They freeze.

Jack flips the light switch.

Evan and Mary stand there, blinking.

I feel angry, and betrayed.

And, yes, I'm scared. What the hell has been going on, *under my roof?*

"M OM —J ACK , IT'S NOT WHAT YOU THINK ," M ARY INSISTS.

I cross my arms at my chest. "Do tell."

"I…screwed up." Tears well in Mary's eyes. "As it turns out, Evan was able to get me out of a jam."

Jack puts his hand on her shoulder. "Start from the beginning."

Mary nods, but drops her head. Her tears fall on her chest. "I played ball with the others, for a half hour or so after you dropped me off. When we went inside, I noticed no one else was there. I asked to be introduced to Sara's mother, but she giggled and said her mother wasn't there. Apparently Sara's older sister was really who you talked to. Her parents are out of town." She gulps down her guilt. "I know I should have called you right then and there to ask to be picked up, but I thought all you wanted to know was that an adult was at the house. Since Sara's sister is twenty, I thought you might not mind."

"You thought wrong. I specifically asked if Sara's mother —not her sister—was going to be there with you."

"I know…Mom, believe me: I wish I had known! When we got bored hanging at her house, Sara's sister dropped us at Hilldale Mall. Sara wanted to walk through the jewelry and make-up departments in Saks Fifth Avenue. I didn't realize that, as I was testing makeup and looking at earrings, she and the other girls were slipping stuff into my purse—a couple of scarves, some bracelets, and expensive lipstick. When we got outside the store, one of the items must have tripped the security alarm, because someone yelled for me to stop. The other girls scattered. Sara shouted, 'You're on your own, kid!'" The tears come faster. "At first, I froze. I couldn't figure out why we were being chased. Then I saw one of the scarves hanging out of my purse. I knew if I got caught, I'd be in big trouble—not only with you, but I'd be tossed off the basketball team, so I threw it on the ground and I ran off too. I hid in the cinema multiplex, in one of the fullest theaters. From there, I called Evan and asked him to pick me up."

"Aunt Phyllis was asleep," Evan offers up. "I know I should have woke her, but Jeff was already in bed too, so I took Aunt Phyllis's Beetle."

Jack and I look at each other. Neither of us noticed that her car wasn't parked on the curb.

Jack shrugs. In other words, Mary and Evan's consequences are my call.

I look at Evan. "I know why you didn't call us. You understand the nature of our work."

He nods emphatically.

"However, you were under the supervision of another adult. Yes, you should have awakened Aunt Phyllis. Evan, what if a policeman had stopped you? You're driving with a learner's permit, which means a fully licensed driver of legal age has to be in the car with you! And if you'd already picked up Mary, both of you would have been hauled into the police station."

"At that point, they may have discovered the items you stole," Jack points out.

"I'm sorry," Evan murmurs.

"You're smart, and we love you. But if you're to live under our roof, you must live by our rules. If you can't do that, we need to know now, Evan."

"No, I—I mean, yes, I want to stay! I want your trust."

"At this point, you'll have to do what you can to earn it back." I turn to Mary. "As for you, I'd like to hear what you feel are the consequences for all this."

Mary purses her lips. "You were right. Sara, Cara, and Tara aren't my friends."

"Why do you say that now?"

She blushes. "Because they encouraged me to ignore your rules, which is the same as lying."

"And why do you think they put you in jeopardy like that, inside the store?"

"Because…well, because they really are bit—I mean selfish, mean girls."

She had it right the first time. "I agree with you about that. Do you think it may have something to do with the fact that being caught shoplifting would have gotten you thrown off the team?"

"I…I guess you're right." Her eyes harden at the realization of what she may have lost.

"Now, why would they want you off the team?"

Her face turns beet red. "Because…well, because Sara thinks Evan and I are…are an item."

Evan looks away, but mumbles, "She's right."

"Wait…" Mary stares at him. "You mean, you know about how she feels about you?"

"Heck yeah. But no way! Everyone knows she's a skank." He shakes his head. "Frankly, I'm glad you've come to your senses about her. I don't want the other guys to think that you—well, that you're anything like her."

Mary smiles shyly. "Thanks, Evan. I guess I should be as concerned about my reputation as you are." She sighs. "I just kept hoping that she'd like me enough not to make my life miserable on the team."

"Besides Sara and her besties, there are nine other girls on the team you can hang with. My guess is those girls have also found out the hard way that she's not much of a friend."

Mary flinches because she knows I'm right.

"I'm glad you want to stay on the team, and that you aren't going to let Sara push you out." I take Mary's hand. "And I'm certainly going to have a talk with her mother. Coach Lonergan should know about her antics too."

Mary frowns. "But—but then Coach Lonergan will know about the theft. And, as far as she or Mrs. Lowell is concerned, it will be Sara's word against mine as to who stole all that stuff! And the other girls will back her up!" Tears glisten in her eyes. "Our first game is tomorrow! If Coach believes Sara, I won't get to play regardless of the truth."

"Any suggestions?" I ask Jack.

"Donna, I'll return the merchandise. It's all tagged as belonging to the store. I'll say I found it on a bench in the park outside the mall. No harm, no foul." His gaze shifts to Mary. "Go to practice. Do your best on the court. Above all, avoid these girls. They're smart enough to figure out that you now know where you stand with them, so their next move is to do everything they can to get under your skin. *Just ignore them.*"

She nods emphatically.

"We'll both be at the game," I tell her. "I promise."

"Thanks, Mom." She hugs me tightly.

Evan nudges her. "We better get some sleep."

Jack and I watch as they walk up the stairs. When they get to Mary's door, Evan gives her a quick hug before taking off down the hall to his own room.

Mary watches until he closes his door. She wipes away a tear before entering her own room.

Jack puts his arm around me. "We should get to bed too."

I rise on my toes to kiss him.

Then I take his hand and we walk up the steps together.

Sure, we'll sleep, but later. I've missed him too much.

11

Erosion

Erosion is the wearing away, washing away, or removal of your garden's topsoil, along with its organic matter, beneficial microorganisms, and nutrients. The most common causes are heavy wind, too much water, or too much human ignorance (that could be any one of us).

To stop erosion, you must devise a way to stabilize the soil, and divert whatever is affecting it. For example:

If it's water, you can add riprap (loose stone), which will slow and divert the flow.

If it's wind, you can terrace the land in a stair-step pattern, to veer off any updraft.

If it's manmade, a shovel to the back of the head of the man responsible will resolve the problem! And, of course, you'll know where to bury him.

(In your garden, silly!)

THE FACE ON THE FOOD AND BEVERAGE MANAGER AT Disneyland is pocked with so many zits that I have to resist the urge to stop and pat him on the head and say, *Don't worry, when you grow up, you'll look fine,* if for no other reason than he may dock my pay for insubordination.

Worse yet, I may lose my "clean workspace" bonus.

I guess I'll have to forfeit it anyway, because as soon as Jack and I secure the corn to be delivered to Frontierland's Corn Cob Chuck Wagon, we're out of here.

The poor kid's name is Bunky Witherspoon. From the look on his oily face, he pities us just as much, as he presumes a minimum wage Disneyland job is the best two thirty-somethings can get.

The chuck wagon looks like an old-school food truck, if you went to school in California around eighteen-seventy. It's even pulled into the park by a team of twenty mules.

And lucky us, our jobs include the tasks of giving the mules water and corn for feed. The worst part: we're in charge of emptying their poopy diapers.

No wonder Bunky feels sorry for us.

Besides our requisite uniforms (khaki pants, large-buckled belts, pointy-toe cowboy boots, button-down denim shirts with Bolo ties), since we're handling food, we must also wear hairnets under our ten-gallon hats, and, of course, thick plastic gloves, but ours are brown, and sport fringe along the cuffs, so that they look like buckskin.

Unbeknownst to Bunky, we've replaced our fake Smith &

Wesson six-shooters with our Sigs. If the last forty-eight hours has taught us anything, it's to never presume that the rest of this mission will be a mop-up-and-done kind of job.

"Okay, so, there's really not much to running the chuck wagon," Bunky assures us. "You boil the corn"—he points to the stove with two industrial-sized burners, where the water in two humongous vats is already percolating—"then you grab them with these tongs"—he lifts a pair that are at least two feet long—"and then you roll it in whatever crap they want"—he points to pans holding various toppings: jalapeño powder, butterscotch, fruit chutney, mayo-chili-cheese, guacamole, nutty curry, and plain old melted butter —"and on the plate it goes." He looks at his watch. "The delivery van should be here any moment now, with today's shipment of fresh corn. I'd help you unload, but I've got to skedaddle. We've got a couple of new employees in the Hamburger Hut. Believe it or not, they're even older than you!"

"Imagine that," Jack mutters wryly.

"Only they're part-timers. Otherwise, they may lose their Social Security checks. I guess that would be a bummer."

You betcha. I resist the urge to point out to him that an even bigger bummer is being sixty-five and having to work the same part-time job you had at eighteen.

"Oops! You've already got a line-up. Better get serving!" He heads off toward another land where quote-unquote dreams come true.

The line is made up of four mothers, accompanied by six children, whose ages vary from about eight to twelve.

Just then, a van pulls up to the chuck wagon. The driver and another man jump out.

I nudge Jack. "Help them unload, while I take care of these customers."

He nods and hops out of the wagon while I turn to answer one of the mother's questions as to whether the jalapeño flavoring is too spicy for her ten-year-old daughter. "Um…I'd play it safe and pass." I point to the photo on the awning of a butter pat melting on a sun-bright yellow ear of corn.

"Okay, then the butterscotch topping for her."

I pull a steaming cob out of the vat, put it on a plate, slather it with the goop, and hand it to her. "Anything else?"

"I think I'd like another one for me, but make it buttered." She purses her lips in thought. "Wait—is it real butter, or a butter substitute?"

"Lady, this is Disneyland. Nothing here is real," I remind her.

"Oh yeah, right." She wrinkles her brow. "How much saturated fat does it contain?"

I look at the now half-mile-long line forming behind her and mutter, "Enough that you should pass."

She angles her head so that she can get a good look at my backside and winces. "I see what you mean. I'll take it plain."

Grrrr.

I plop another boiling corncob onto a plate for her. I hope it burns her tongue.

The next Mom bemoans the fact that her son wants the

nutty chutney. "But he's got so many food allergies. What kind of nuts is used?"

"Um…peanuts."

"How about the chili? Does it have MSG?"

Hell if I know. "Yes," I answer emphatically.

She sighs. "Well, then that just won't do! Okay, let me have two, buttered."

I place two steaming cobs on plates, and slather them with the butter sauce. But just as I'm about to hand them off to the woman, from behind me Jack proclaims, "I've got it! Twenty bags of Exodus corn, all accounted for!"

To prove it, he raises a cob of the killer corn from the neck of one of the bags.

The woman cranes her neck to see what all the commotion is about. "Oh! If that's fresher, we'll wait for it instead."

Yowch. "Quite frankly, it's all the same."

"But that corn is still in its husks. It's got to be fresher!" She folds her arms over her chest. "I'd prefer to wait," she says in a very loud voice.

"I would too," the mother behind her declares. She turns to the rest of the crowd and shouts, "They've just had a delivery of fresher corn. Wouldn't you prefer to wait for it?"

Her proclamation garners nods all up and down the line, along with chants of "Fresh-*ER!* Fresh-*ER!* Fresh-*ER!*"

"What do you think we should do?" Jack mutters in my ear.

"Get the hell out of Dodge," I hiss back. I nod toward the wagon's coach seat, where the reins to the mule team are tied.

I don't have to ask him twice.

In no time at all, the mules are hoofing it toward Main Street, USA.

The crowd parts for us. The toothy grins of enthralled children turn our way. Clasped to the bosoms of their parents, they wave to us as our braying steeds clip-clop right through the cast members' gate of "the happiest place on Earth."

"GOOD JOB SEIZING THOSE ASSETS," RYAN SAYS. "BUT DID YOU have to leave the damn mules in the Disneyland employee parking lot?" He points to the conference room monitor, where a newsman is reporting on what he describes as "an unusual incident."

Jack rolls his eyes. "I guess we could have brought them here."

"No! No, that's not what I meant," Ryan bats the suggestion away. "Okay, maybe I'm being a bit picky. But our mandate has been to keep this mission under the radar."

"We're doing the best we can, under the circumstances," I point out as I plop down in the chair beside him. "Only two more seizures—at Fizz Cola and TasTee Cereals—and we're home free."

"When's the next shipment due to arrive?" he asks.

"Tonight, at TasTee. We know this because Arnie has hacked the phone of the owner, Glory Buchanan," Jack replies. "It's a small operation. She sells exclusively to health food grocery stores. She makes her deliveries during the day. At night, her supposedly organically-grown cereals are made by hand."

"How did it end up on Wellborne's list?" I wonder out loud.

"Nothing in the distribution of the Exodus seeds happened by chance. If word of the killer corn had gotten out, organic food products made of corn would be flying off the shelves, with people assuming the organic products were safe. Can you imagine the panic if people thought that the killer corn had also been utilized in organic foods?"

"It would be pretty crazy! People wouldn't know what food they could trust," I murmur.

"Hey, was Arnie able to trace the source of the funds dropped into Wellborne's Caymans account?" Jack asks.

"He's still working on it, and so is Dominic—supposedly." Ryan grimaces. "Or I should say, he's working on the bank's private accounts manager. Not that I can blame him for suggesting that he go at the issue from, as he put it, 'a different angle'."

Ryan's screen shifts to a photo of a tall, gorgeous Native Islander in a string bikini. Dominic's camera watch must have taken a picture just as she bent over to rub her legs with tanning lotion.

Jack chuckles. "Yes, I can imagine that angle is the most irresistible, from Dominic's perspective."

"I told him he's got twenty-four hours to get something out of her," Ryan growls.

"Really, *that* long?" I say rolling my eyes. "I'd give him, say twenty seconds, tops."

My pun doesn't sink in immediately. When finally it does, Jack laughs so hard that he tears up.

Ryan is only a second or two behind Jack. I've never seen him so red.

I guess that's why he waves us out of the conference room with the command, "Find someone else to bother."

JACK IS PICKING UP TRISHA FROM SCHOOL, WHILE I GRAB JEFF. Then we'll meet up at Hilldale High School to watch Mary's first game playing for the girls' varsity basketball team.

As I pull up to the front of Hilldale Middle School, I notice that there is a man standing with Jeff. He is tall and dark-skinned.

I pull over and park, then get out of the car. Jeff spots me and waves.

The man walks over with him. "I'd like to introduce myself," he says. "I'm Mr. Karman."

"Ah! Jeff's Current Events teacher." I hold out my hand for him to shake. "I'm Donna Stone. Is everything alright?"

"I hope so," Mr. Karman says. "It seems that Jeff wants to transfer out of my class to a similar one taught by one of my colleagues. I'm perplexed at the request, considering his exemplary grades to date and his easy engagement in the topic, both with me and with his classmates." He looks down at Jeff. Frustration lines Mr. Karman's face.

I look down at my son. "Jeff, is there a particular reason as to why you'd like to make the move?"

"I feel…Well…" Embarrassed, he bows his head. "Mom, I just feel it's the best move for me."

I'm not as convinced, but obviously, it's something Jeff does not want to discuss with Mr. Karman, or for that matter, in front of him.

I put my hands on his shoulders. "Mr. Karman, Jeff and I will discuss it tonight. He'll give you his decision tomorrow."

Mr. Karman nods sadly. I can see he'd hoped to enlist me immediately as his ally.

"Jeff, the car door is open," I point out. "Go ahead and take a seat. I'd like a moment with Mr. Karman."

He nods, grabs his backpack, and hurries to the car.

I wait until he shuts the door, then I turn to Mr. Karman. "I can imagine you find this distressing. Believe me, it's a total surprise to me as well. I was under the impression that he enjoyed your class tremendously." I hesitate then add, "Frankly, he's been able to work out some personal issues he has with world affairs through his research of topics that most trouble him."

"Yes, the whole school was saddened by his personal experience with terrorism." He looks me in the eye. "I want you to know it was Jeff's idea to choose terrorism as his paper's topic. I was surprised. Still, I'd hoped the adage, 'knowledge is power,' would be a soothing balm for his emotional wounds. But now…" He shakes his head sadly. "As it turns out, he's not the only student to request a transfer."

I can guess whom: Cheever and Morton.

"Until recently, I've met with little bigotry in Hilldale." He sighs. "Should it continue, I may give up teaching." He lifts his head proudly. "The loss will be the children's as well as mine. The more they interact with people from other parts of the world, the more they understand how big our world really is—and how lucky they are to live here, in the United States."

"I cannot agree more," I assure him. "I'll do my best with Jeff to have him see your perspective, both as a teacher and a mentor."

"I'd appreciate that, Mrs. Stone." He bows slightly then takes his leave.

"I DON'T HATE HIM," JEFF SAYS.

Other than that one comment, our first mile in the car together was silent. In truth, I didn't know what to say to my son. Now I'm glad I let him speak first.

"You seemed to enjoy his class. You're getting wonderful grades in it. And I presume you've learned a lot. So, why make a transfer out?"

"Because he may be a terrorist." Jeff's voice trembles.

I glance over at him. "Jeff, what makes you say that?"

"He...he takes calls in private. Also, that thing that Cheever said—you know, about seeing him pray during lunch hour."

"Jeff, all people—no matter where they're from—have different customs. And every religion is different in how it is practiced and in regard to its traditions. You can be devout in your religious beliefs without being a terrorist." I sigh. "Please don't buy into Cheever and Mrs. Bing's paranoia."

"I'm not! I swear!" Jeff frowns. "Mom, Mr. Karman sent my paper to someone else!"

"How do you know this?" I ask.

"Because I saw him do it. He went to the faculty copier room with it. When he was done, he put it in a manila envelope. The man's name was Arabic too"—he closes his eyes as he thinks. "It was Abdul Al-Salami."

"What is Mr. Al-Salami's address?"

Jeff shrugs. "It was all I could read. I…well, I ducked when Mr. Karman turned my way."

With what Jeff went through, I can see why Mr. Karman's act might alarm him. "Okay, Jeff, I defer to your gut feelings on this situation. In the meantime, I'll do some research on both Mr. Karman and Mr. Al-Salami, if only to put your mind at ease, one way or another."

Jeff's way of thanking me is to kiss me on the cheek.

By the time I pull into the Hilldale High School gym's parking lot, both of us have dried our tears.

I text Emma the two names, adding: *No rush, but when you get around to it.*

The way the Exodus mission is going, that may be never.

12

Sucker

The term "sucker" is used to describe plant growth—say, a sprout—originating from the rootstock of a grafted plant, rather than the desired part of the plant.

Sucker growth should be removed, so it doesn't draw energy from the main stalk of the plant.

Humans are sometimes also described as suckers. This occurs when they are duped into doing something that makes them look foolish.

Should someone try to make a sucker out of you, feel free to remove their head from their body. That way, they don't draw energy from your life.

THE HILLDALE HIGH SCHOOL GIRLS VARSITY BASKETBALL TEAM

tears out onto the court to the *Rocky* theme, like Amazons ready to do battle with lesser beings.

That is, everyone but Mary. She takes up the rear and fairly stumbles out. When she is halfway across the court, she rubs her eyes, as if waking up from an afternoon nap.

I know she came in late, but still, she had plenty of shut-eye. What could be wrong with her?

The air is charged with the exhilaration that only comes from a local rivalry, such as Hilldale's with today's competitor, the Newport Harbor High School Sailors. Add to this the fate of the regional title and you can understand why the bleachers are wall-to-wall anxiety.

Thank goodness Evan saved everyone seats, on the aisle of the center column of seats, in the last row. Aunt Phyllis is already here too.

I kiss her cheek. "I thought you'd be here later. Didn't you have an art class earlier this afternoon?"

"Yes. We're painting nudes, and some of those guys are hung." She sighs appreciatively. "As tempting as that is, I wouldn't have missed Mary's first varsity game for anything in the world."

While the other girls are already going through their warm-up drills—tossing free-throws through the end-court hoop, passing basketballs up and down a drill line, and dribbling in figure-eights and cross-overs—Mary stands there, twirling a strand of hair around her middle finger. Finally, Coach Lonergan runs over to her. Whatever her coach is saying has Mary nodding her head vigorously, and running over to join her teammates, who are dribbling.

Her own moves are less than stellar, if not downright embarrassing. She loses her ball at least four times. Not only that, she misses four out of five hoop shots.

Each time it happens, Sara nudges Cara, who nudges Tara.

I hate seeing them enjoying her distress.

"What's wrong with Mary?" Jeff asks.

"Beats me," Evan answers. He's so worried that he paces the bleacher behind us.

Trisha covers her eyes with her hands.

I feel like doing the same. *Something is very, very wrong.*

When the ref blows the whistle, the players run to their respective sideline benches—

Except for Mary. She heads off in the wrong direction. When she realizes what she's done, she flips around, but the crowd is already laughing. She turns beet red as she shuffles to her seat on the bench.

If her teammates aren't staring at her, they're angrily inching away from her.

It's going to be one heck of a long game.

I CAN'T BLAME THE COACH FOR KEEPING MARY SIDELINED UNTIL the last few minutes of the game, considering that my daughter has barely moved from whatever zombie state she's in. Why is she catatonic? Has making the varsity team been too overwhelming?

When she finally gets pulled off the bench, it's only

because Hilldale's lead is ten points, and state rules are such that she has to be played, if only for a few minutes. But her footwork is lethargic at best, comical at worst.

Still, she manages to get right under the basket. And in that instant, Cara passes her the ball. Mary dribbles and shoots—

Right over the backstop.

The crowd roars with laughter.

Thank goodness the buzzer goes off.

While the other girls shake hands with the losing team, Mary stands under the basket, frozen in her humiliation.

When Sara and her posse pass her, they jostle her so hard that she falls to the floor. She has to crawl before she stands up.

Jack and I lead the family in a trot from the bleachers to where she sits. Evan beats us to her.

Her eyes are damp, but the tears don't seem to fall. Jack helps her to her feet. She walks to the car with her head bowed. "I'm sorry. I screwed up," she whispers. "Please— take me home."

"Your clothes and books—where are they?"

She shrugs. "My backpack…is in my gym locker."

"I'll get it for you," Evan offers. "Bay G, locker number fourteen-ninety-two, and the combination: it's four-one-five- four-one-five, right?"

She stares up at him. "How did you know?"

"Don't you remember? A couple of weeks ago, you left your library book at school by mistake. I was still here, so I brought it home with me."

She nods absently. "Yeah…I remember…I think."

"Go on home with Jack and Trisha," I tell Mary. "Jeff, Evan, and I will bring it with us."

I watch as Jack puts his arm around her and leads her out of the gym.

"That wasn't Mary out there," Evan insists.

"I know what you mean." I throw up my hands. "Maybe the pressure of playing her first game got to her, coupled with all the head games played on her by those mean girls. But whether it was or wasn't, it's what her coach will judge her on. I'll move the car to the front of the gym. Meet us there after you grab her gear."

Evan nods as he trots off toward the gym.

Jeff shakes his head angrily. "Mom, that's not fair to her! Just because she screwed up once—"

"Jeff, I agree wholeheartedly. Still, it's not our decision to make. We have to prepare her for the possibility that she may be released from the team."

Jeff shrugs.

It's not until I'm halfway across the gym floor that I notice Jeff isn't following.

When I turn back around, I notice he's sitting back in the bleachers. He's pulled out his laptop. "I'll meet you at the car in a minute!" he shouts. He waves me off.

Homework…now?

I start to object, but what's the use?

I head to the parking lot.

By the time we get home, Mary is up in her room with the door closed.

"She's sleeping," Jack tells us.

"I'm glad." I plop down in the kitchen banquette beside Jeff. He's still on his laptop. He hasn't looked up from it since we left the gym.

"After the game, I wanted to take everyone out for pizza," Jack says. "But since Mary isn't in the mood to celebrate, I asked Aunt Phyllis and Trisha went to pick up Chinese food instead."

"Great idea." I sigh. "Although, I don't think anyone has much of an appetite."

Evan holds up Mary's gym bag. "Should I take this up to her room?"

"Leave it with me." I hold out my hand. "I'll throw her gym clothes in with the wash."

When I open it, I'm met with the sweet and sour smells of sweaty clothes, socks, and sneakers. I pull them out, but leave her deodorant, liquid soap, shampoo, hair conditioner, comb, brush and moisturizer in the bag. Her water bottle is also in the bag. It's only half-full, so I take it to the sink to empty it. I've unscrewed the twist top and I'm just about to pour it out when Jeff yells, "Mom—*don't!*"

I freeze, then turn to him. "What's the matter?"

"We may want to keep it as evidence." He motions me over to his computer screen.

I come closer to find myself looking at a row of gym lockers. The banner hanging on the wall proclaims *GO HILL-DALE WILDCATS!*

"What is this?" I ask.

"The security footage by Mary's locker."

I stare down at him. "Jeff, how did you get this?"

"I hacked into the school's database. I've watched Emma do it a few times—you know, when she worked out of the bonus room over the garage. Look, I know it's illegal unless you've got a permit, but this is important, right? Mary shouldn't be kicked off the team because she was drugged!"

He points to the screen.

Darned if he's not right.

The time stamp is one-thirty, which would make it prior to the game.

Sara, Cara and Tara walk up to the lockers. While the other girls stand guard, Sara works the combination until it opens. She then unzips Mary's gym bag and pulls out Mary's baby blue water canister. She takes off the screw top, and pours something out of a tiny envelope into the bottle. She screws the top on, shakes it, puts the canister back in the gym bag, and closes the locker, twirling the lock in place. The girls run off, giggling.

After a ten minute time lapse, Mary can be seen at the locker, taking out her bag. She's yet to put on her basketball team uniform.

The first thing she does is to take a swig from the bottle before hurrying off.

"Was Mary dumb enough to give them her combination number?"

"I doubt it," Evan insists. Suddenly, his face goes white. "When she called me about her library book, she was with

Sara and the others. I could hear them in the background. Maybe they overheard her."

"My guess is that you're right." I stick my nose into the bottle and take a sniff. "I can't smell anything, but that doesn't mean anything."

"If it's a roofie, it wouldn't have an odor, anyway," Evan points out.

"Even if it turned the water blue, since her canister is that color anyway, Mary would not have noticed," I add.

"After dinner, we'll take this to Acme. Ryan can run a chemical analysis. We can leave for TasTee from there," Jack suggests.

"Mom, you're not mad at me, are you?" Jeff asks.

I shake my head, but say, "No—*but don't do it again.*"

"Until you grow up and work for Acme," Jack mutters.

I smack his arm and hiss, "Bite your tongue."

"This is my fault!" Evan exclaims. "All I had to do was go out with Sara, and she would have left Mary alone. Sara humiliated her to get even with me."

I squeeze his hand. "Sara is one sick puppy. Kowtowing to her would not have affected how she feels about Mary. Just knowing how close you are would have been reason enough to hurt her. Her vindictiveness comes out of her insecurity and jealousies."

"Just like my mother," he mutters. "Maybe that's why I've tried to stay clear of her."

I almost say, *Then you have good sense.*

Instead, I hold my tongue.

Evan still hasn't given us his decision regarding the trip

to see his mother. We still have a few days before he tells me one way or another, but based on what he just said, my guess is that he'll pass.

Suddenly, I've lost my appetite.

THE HOT PINK COTTAGE THAT HOUSES TASTEE CEREALS IS IN A tidy little neighborhood on the outskirts of East Pasadena.

A sign on the front door reads: ALL DELIVERIES ARE MADE VIA ALLEY IN BACK.

We set up there: Jack and I pull up just beyond the driveway in front of the house, while Abu, in an unmarked van, sits at the mouth of the dead-end alley. After the truck pulls in, Abu will block the alley. He's got a dashboard camera ready to record the delivery and the driver's arrest. We can hear each other through our earbuds, as can Emma back at Acme headquarters.

The intel Emma pulled up on it shows the company's revenues to be under five million dollars, all earned through small independent grocery chains, as well as health food stores. The press on the product is more than decent. Photos of Glory Buchanan show a woman in her fifties who wears flowing muumuus printed in a psychedelic swirl of colors, her long, flowing hair is a deep brown, except at her widow's peak, which is stark white. Her large eyes are soft brown in color.

TasTee's website is filled with ecstatic customer reviews. "It's nothing like we've ever tasted," proclaims Jen Tucker of

Lafayette, Indiana. Francine LaSala of North Hills, New York exclaims, "You can taste the freshness in every bite!" These accolades go on for several pages.

A banner at the top of the website announces: *Coming Soon! Best. TasTee Flakes. Ever!*

Seeing this, I murmur to Jack, "I guess Barnaby did a real hard sell to get her to sign on to the Exodus corn. She must have known he only deals in GMO earlage."

Jack shrugs. "He's a snake charmer. I wouldn't put anything past him, especially if he followed Wellborne's mandate: to slip it into the food chain in as many ways as possible."

I shudder at the thought.

The waiting game begins.

AN HOUR GOES BY AND STILL NO TRUCK.

Finally, I say, "Why don't we knock on the door and see what's up?"

Jack nods. "Good idea. Abu, let us know if the truck rolls up, and we'll come right out."

"Will do."

THE WINDOW THROUGH THE BACK DOOR IS COVERED IN A SHEER curtain. There seems to be no activity inside.

Our first knock goes unanswered.

Our second elicits a moan from somewhere inside.

"Did you hear that?" Jack asks.

I nod. I try the doorknob, but it's locked.

Jack picks it. If need be, we'll explain later.

THE WHOLE HOUSE SMELLS OF BURNT CORN.

We find Glory Buchanan lying face down on the floor of the kitchen.

Jack and I kneel over her. "Glory? Glory, what's wrong?"

"Head…hurts," she whispers.

Jack lifts her gently in his arms, and walks her down the hall to a bedroom.

"They've come and gone. Call FDA HazMat," I order Emma.

I look around. The space is set up like an industrial kitchen with a triple-sink wash station, an eight-burner range, and triple ovens.

About twenty bags of earlage are stacked in one corner.

One bag is open, and two-thirds empty. Cobs taken from it have already been husked, and kernels have been shaved.

A large food processor sits on top of one of the food prep stations. A large bowl of kernels sits under it.

Cookie sheets are still in one of the ovens, their flakes burning to cinders.

On another prep station, toasted flakes sit on a giant cookie sheet. An eighth of the flakes are gone.

I find them in a bowl, soggy with milk.

I turn off the ovens, but I touch nothing.

I run to the bedroom where Glory is laid out. "She ate the corn," I tell Jack.

She's mumbling deliriously.

He slaps her face gently. "Glory…can you speak? When did you get the corn?"

"Mor…morning." Her eyes pop open. Incoherent phrases tumble out of her mouth, "paper…dirty fingers… corn…colors…*bad?*"

I shake my head in awe. "Does this crap work that fast?"

He shrugs. "You saw the cows."

Four minutes later, an FDA HazMat battalion—two vans and an ambulance—roll down the alley.

We get out of the way.

WE'RE PULLING INTO HILLDALE WHEN WE GET A CALL FROM Ryan. "Despite numerous attempts of resuscitation, Glory Buchanan expired five minutes ago."

"Thanks for the update." I suddenly realize how stupid it sounds to thank someone for the news of an innocent victim's death.

When we enter the house, we see that Aunt Phyllis is watching the news. "Oh, my God! There's a five-alarm fire in East Pasadena!" She points at the TV screen. "I hope it doesn't blow over in the direction of my house."

The news reporter's camera shows flames shooting out of the roof of Glory's bungalow.

Jack looks at me, but says nothing. I know what he's thinking: the cleanup crew is taking care of one last bit of business.

We head upstairs to catch a few hours of sleep.

I RISE AT FIVE.

Jack is still lying beside me, but his eyes are open. He pulls me in close, for a kiss.

We hit the shower together. In no time, a cocoon of steam envelops us.

We stand there in each other's arms. I could stay this way all day.

But, no, there's still work to do.

We head downstairs to find Mary sitting at the kitchen table. Wanly, she waves at us.

She doesn't wave us away when we come to hug her. "Mom, what happened at the game yesterday?" she whispers. "Why don't I remember anything?"

Then, while Jack makes waffles, I tell her what really happened.

Slowly, the rest of our brood makes their way downstairs. No one speaks through my monologue, but when I mention the role Jeff played, Mary gives her brother a kiss. When I tell her Evan's supposition on how Sara got her locker combination, she squeezes his hand.

In return, he does more than that: he kisses her forehead, but then backs away quickly.

They are both embarrassed by his action.

Not me. I cherish their friendship with each other.

When I'm done, Mary says nothing, but shakes her head for a full minute. Finally, she gets up and angrily paces the room. I watch as a myriad of emotions play out in the muscles in her face: disbelief, realization, hurt, anger—only to settle into stoic resignation. She releases her tension with a long sigh. "Even with this evidence, we can't snitch on them."

"Why not?" Jack, Jeff, Evan and I exclaim in unison.

"Because if the three best players we have get suspended, it will demoralize the team—and…they'll still hate me for it."

"That's not your call to make. It belongs to your coach and your principal." I look her straight in the eye. "Ethics aside, do you know what kind of liability these girls have imposed on the school? What if the drug had caused an adverse effect, like a coma—or your death?"

Jack takes her hand. "And, Mary, in regard to the rest of the team, ask yourself: if you'd discovered that three team-mates had done this to another, would you want to play with them?"

Mary recoils. "No! Never!"

"So, why would you think the others would feel differently?" Jack asks.

"I guess you're right." She bites her bottom lip. "Okay, then, I guess we should talk to Coach Lonergan."

"You should take the day to rest," I insist. "I'll call the

school and let the administration know you're staying home today."

"I'll look after our big girl," Aunt Phyllis declares. "Chicken soup, hot cocoa—oh! And we'll binge-watch the whole season of *The Bachelor*!"

Mary smiles wanly.

"Jack and I have to go out this morning, but I'll be home before school lets out. By then, Acme's lab will have screened the contents of your water bottle. If what we suspect is true, we'll show it to Coach Lonergan." I smooth her hair in order to have an excuse to touch my sweet girl. "Part of growing up is making hard decisions, even if they aren't popular."

Mary's grin fades, but she nods her head. She knows it won't be an easy conversation, but she also realizes that it's the best decision all the way around.

13

Pinching Back

To promote a bushier plant, try "pinching back"—that is, nipping off—the very tip of a branch, or a stem. You do this by clipping it between your thumb and forefinger.

You can also pinch back a relationship that is less than desirable. However, it won't be accomplished merely with a flick of your thumb and forefinger. Perhaps not even with the rise of your middle finger.

Instead, start with some sort of paralysis drug that leaves the person in question—let's call her Nosybody—limp and placid. Next, slam Nosybody's head against a concrete floor—perhaps three times. This should leave Nosybody with severe fractures.

At that point, if you want to saw off Nosybody's head, go for it. But, frankly, it's overkill.

(Hmmm, "overkill." Really, is there such a thing in the case of Nosybodies?)

Abu is trailing us to Santa Ana in an unmarked Acme van. Fizz Cola can be found in a warehouse district on the west side of town.

We're a half-hour from the town's first highway exit when Ryan's call comes through. He waits until Abu is patched in too before saying, "So that we can pinpoint the time of the TasTee delivery and the vehicle that made it, Arnie has been pulling yesterday morning's archival data off the city of Pasadena's street cams."

Arnie's voice is the next one we hear on my cell phone's speaker. "It's taken me all night and up until ten minutes ago, but I think I've struck gold. A plain white large panel van is seen heading down the alley at about eight-seventeen, yesterday morning. It heads back out approximately twenty minutes later."

"Did you grab the plate number?" Abu asks.

"Yes," he replies. "I've just texted you a photo of it. But if this guy is smart enough to dump his burner phones after each text and to mask its GPS, I presume he's got a closet full of stolen plates, too."

"And, don't forget, the amount of corn needed at Fizz is at least ten times more than what TasTee ordered. In all likelihood, a different vehicle is being used."

"Duly noted," Jack and Abu say in unison.

"Speaking of security feeds," I chime in, "Arnie, can you hack into Fizz's webcam? If the driver made the TasTee delivery earlier than anticipated, he could he have done the same in the case of Fizz. Check for a delivery of corn being made within the last twenty-four hours."

"Damn it! I should have thought of that," Arnie mutters. He mutes the phone for a moment. When he comes back to us, he exclaims, "Got it! I'll split this up amongst the team, so that we can get back to you, pronto." The next thing we hear is Arnie shouting, "Emma, rustle up a couple of techs to fast-forward through some B-roll with me!"

By the time he calls back, we're parked in front of the Fizz bottling plant. "The delivery was made at three this morning. It's a black eighteen-wheeler with no markings. The plate was stolen off a Walmart truck." He texts us the license plate number: *6JMB415*.

"Now that we're here, what's our Plan B?" I ask.

"Wing it," Jack says, half-jokingly.

"I've got a better idea," Arnie says. "I've just hacked into Fizz's security cam feed, and followed the trajectory of the corn. The plant has already processed it into syrup. The various flavoring oils have been added to it, as well as seltzer, sugar, and coloring elements. As we speak, it's about to be bottled." We hear him tapping out something on his computer. "I've just texted each of you an employee badge barcode that identifies you as three people who called in sick this morning."

"Got it," I reply.

Arnie has also sent us a schematic of the bottling machine. "Thank goodness this plant doesn't also use cans, or you'd really be running around."

"You mean, we're not already?" Jack smirks.

I poke him. "Keep talking, Arnie."

"Well, ideally, you'll be able to drain the syrup vat before it even hits the first bottle."

"And if we can't?" Abu asks.

"I guess that would be Plan C—that is, stop the plastic bottles, which are pressurized before they reach the filling room, from being infused with cola. The cola going in them is chilled to a temperature of thirty-six degrees Fahrenheit. Otherwise it would go flat. Now here's the tricky part: the machine fills eight hundred bottles a minute. And to retain the pressure, the filled bottles are immediately capped, then labeled, and then lassoed into packaging. Usually a case-worth—that is twelve bottles—is wrapped in a plastic coat—"

"Too much information, Arnie!" I exclaim impatiently.

"No," he says, miffed. "All of this is very important, in case you need a Plan D, E, F and G."

This time, Jack pokes me. "Okay then, Arnie, please continue."

"As I was saying, all of this is done on a conveyor system that is two miles long. Sometimes the bottles stop in a holding area on the conveyor system. That being said, if you've missed any of the other steps, you can still catch the cases there, after being capped, or shoved into a seven-layer pallet, which is wrapped in plastic. Of course, the very worst case scenario—that is, Plan Z—is that the cola has already been bottled and packaged, so you hijack the truck."

"We're on it," Jack says.

"Um…which part?" Ryan asks.

"All of it. You'll just have to trust us." He hits the off button on the speaker.

TOO MANY PEOPLE ARE FLOATING AROUND FIZZ FOR ANYONE TO question that we belong in the employee dressing room, let alone in the bottling warehouse.

Uniforms consist of full-body coveralls, hairnets, eye goggles, and booties that go over our shoes.

"Have I told you how fetching you look in a hairnet?" Jack asks.

I smile. "You truly know how to flatter a girl."

"You kids are so adorable," Arnie rhapsodizes.

"Cut the crap," Ryan mutters. "Arnie, which vat holds the secret sauce?"

"Vat Number Fourteen. Like I said, we're too late to stop the corn syrup from being mixed with the other ingredients into the cola, and it's up next to be infused into the bottles."

"How do we stop that from happening?" Jack asks.

"There's a release at the bottom of the vat, in case the cola is contaminated in any way. It falls into a holding tank."

"Okay, I'm on it," I say.

"And I'll secure the holding tank until the FDA agents come," Abu assures us.

He runs off in one direction, and I stroll off in another—toward the vats. I climb Vat Fourteen's ladder, as if I know what I'm doing.

"Donna, hurry!" Arnie warns me. The foreman is about to turn on the spigot that releases the syrup into the bottles!"

I double-time it up the stairs—

But even that isn't quick enough. By the time I pull the release on the spigot, half the vat is already empty.

Standing high on a catwalk, the vat foreman spots me. He wags finger and shouts, "Hey—you! Who the hell are you?"

Instead of walking, I slide down the ladder rail. "Some of it got into bottles," I gasp.

"I'll meet you there," Jack replies.

Before the foreman can get on the floor, I disappear behind the conveyor belt.

JACK'S WAY OF STOPPING THE COLA FROM GOING INTO THE bottles is a simple process of elimination: he takes a metal pole and bats a row of plastic bottles from beneath the filler nozzles.

Cola spews all over him. "Damn it, this crap is freezing!"

"Not quite freezing," Arnie corrects him, "but yes, hella cold."

As the bottles go flying, Ryan murmurs, "Home run!"

"You did it, Jack!" Arnie exclaims.

Jack grabs my hand. "Let's get out of here. Sabotaging a bottling plant can kick up an appetite. What do you say to In-N-Out Burger?"

I nod. "Sure—but water, no cola."

I'M STARING OUTSIDE THE WINDOW OF IN-N-OUT BURGER WHEN I see it: a black sixteen-wheeler with the California license plate number of 6JMB415, pulling out of the parking lot of the stripper club next door.

I point out the window, choking on my double-double.

Jack slaps me on the back. "Heimlich! Do you need the Heimlich?"

I point at the truck.

He gets it. He's out the door.

I'm on his heels.

TRAFFIC ON THE SIX-LANE SANTA ANA BOULEVARD IS HEAVY enough that the truck only gets as far as two blocks down the road before it's stopped at another light. From where he's sitting, the only thing to stare at is the filthy backpacker who's standing on the median with a sign that reads SACTO.

The backpacker isn't too happy when I decide to give him some competition. And, since I've already opened all the buttons of my blouse and tied it right below my lace bra, I'd say it's really no contest.

When I hold out my thumb, the driver of the Exodus truck blows me a kiss.

I blow one back, then I toss my head. Because the light is

six seconds from changing, I lick my lips as an incentive to speed along this courtship we've got going.

He takes the hint. Reaching over the cab, he opens the passenger door.

As I hop in, I notice that Backpacker has unbuttoned his flannel shirt and tied the ends together, right below his moobs.

Good luck with that, pal.

"You're a doll," I coo. "Whattya say to pulling over until the traffic lightens up? That way, I can thank you, all proper like." To make my point, I purse my lips.

I don't have to ask twice.

He screeches around the first corner. Lucky us, it's a dead-end alley.

If you've never held a gun under a man's testicles, you should give it a try, just once anyway. He's chattering so hard that it takes me a full five minutes to get him to confess that he knows exactly what he delivered; that, yes, Wellborne paid him to do it; and yes, this is his last delivery.

Jack pulls around the corner, just as I've cuffed the driver's hands.

"What took you so long?" I ask.

"I stopped for these." He holds up a bouquet of pink roses.

He's earned a kiss.

"So, all's well that ends well?"

"Yes," I say emphatically.

"Great. I'll call Abu to swing by and pick me up, along with your new boyfriend. By the way, I've got Mary's water bottle with me, so that he can take it into the Acme lab for content analysis." He tosses me the car keys. "Are you fine with picking up the kids?"

He doesn't have to ask twice. I take my flowers and scram.

First stop: Hilldale Elementary School.

The carpool line is almost at a standstill, what with all the Daisy Scouts rapping on the drivers' windows and asking them to buy yet one more box of cookies, so that the troop can be number one in the state.

"Mommy, we're only a hundred boxes away from first place," Trisha announces, as she hops in the car.

I sigh. "Okay, we'll buy ten more—but that's it."

This earns me a kiss.

Even before I get to Hilldale Middle School, there is a text from the school—unfortunately, from Principal Belding:

See me.

Jeff is in trouble?

I double-time it to the school, swerving toward the curb outside the administration building.

I walk into Mr. Belding's office to find Jeff already there, as well as Cheever and his mother, Penelope Bing. Belding sits behind his desk. There is nothing on it except for a sheaf of papers.

Since I can read pages upside down, I can make out Jeff's name. It's his term paper:

A Comprehensive Look at Terrorism in Today's World

Perhaps Jeff is getting a commendation?

Noting my baffled look, Belding says, "Not to worry, Mrs. Stone. Jeff has shown exemplary work in his Current Events class."

My shoulders relax, as does my frown. "Oh! Well, congratulations, Jeff." I pat him on the shoulder, but he doesn't smile.

So, why is my son so sad?

"Are you aware of the fact that Mr. Karman shared Jeff's paper with an outside source?"

"Um…no," I say softly.

"I thought not," Belding declares. "Unfortunately, in doing so, Mr. Karman broke a cardinal rule of the school."

"Oh. Well…did he have a reason for doing so?" I ask.

"I didn't ask for one," Belding said smugly. "Again, the fact that he did it is reason enough for the immediate termination of his contract."

"Don't concern yourself, Donna," Penelope says smugly. "He was acting strangely in so many other ways, too."

"You mean, using his lunch hour for a private prayer session?" I ask.

Her eyes narrow into tiny slits. "You know about that?"

"Cheever made sure everyone knows…or is that your doing, Penelope? And since when is it a crime to pray behind closed doors?"

She turns bright red under her makeup foundation. "I'm certainly not going to apologize for my concerns in times of terror!" She tosses her frosted mane. "Frankly, if anyone should be on alert, I'd think it would be *you*."

She doesn't know the half of it.

And, frankly, she doesn't have the clearance for me to tell her.

Without another word, I put my arm around Jeff's shoulder and leave.

EMMA CALLS. "CONGRATULATIONS! WOW, TALK ABOUT A CRAZY mission! I'll bet you're happy it's over!"

"Totally," I admit. I cup my ear to the phone and move into the dining room so that I can hear her over Trisha's tallying of her sales to date. "I'm ready to get back to normal. Speaking of which, your Daisy Scout cookies should be here any day now."

"You mean Arnie's order. I'm sure he'll be thrilled."

I laugh. "Not a fan of the cookie, eh?"

"You hit the nail right on the head—too many sweeteners, too many additives, too many fillers, and too many calories!"

"Yes, I've seen Arnie in a bathing suit. It's obvious who has the sweet tooth in your family."

"I've got my fingers crossed that Nicky won't inherit it, but I don't hold out much hope." Emma sighs. "Hey listen, I called for two reasons. First, the water sample you left with Abu to be tested in the lab contains Rohypnol. I've texted you a PDF of the formal lab results."

"Thanks, Emma." So, it's as we suspected.

"Secondly, I finally had a chance to research the connection between the two men you called about a couple of days ago—Omar Karman and Abdul Al-Salami. As it turns out, they went to college together—Stanford. Al-Salami is currently a professor there, in the area of International Studies. Karman is a middle-school teacher—at Jeff's school. Or, I should say, he was."

"Yes, I just found out he's been fired."

"Did you also know he committed suicide?"

I drop into a chair. "Say that again?"

"It happened this afternoon. He hung himself. It was the last thing that popped on him on the United States' Enforcement Integrated Database. His death hasn't made the news yet because LAPD hasn't contacted his next of kin, in Yemen. They may never find them, what with everyone fleeing ISIL over there. It was one of the reasons he wrote about in his suicide note—well, that, being let go from his job, and all the prejudice he'd encountered."

"What he wrote doesn't surprise me at all," I murmur. "Emma, do you have a number for Professor Al-Salami?"

"I have his direct faculty number as well his cell number." She reads them off.

"Thank you for this. Hey, if you need more Daisy Scout cookies—"

She laughs. "You mean, if Arnie needs more cookies! And yes, we know who to call." She's still chuckling as she hangs up.

I've got nothing to laugh about.

I dial the number she gave me.

"Ah, Mrs. Stone! It's almost as if you'd read my mind," exclaims Abdul Al-Salami.

"I... I beg your pardon?"

"A friend of mine—Omar Karman—is a big admirer of your son, Jeff. I can see why. Your son's grasp of the problem of terrorism is incredible. More importantly, the insights he shows in his paper's conclusion are similar to that of many who have been studying the topic for the past decade."

"Professor, why did Mr. Karman share the paper with you?"

Professor Al-Salami chuckles. "He'd hoped to convince me to make an exception for Jeff and offer him a position in Stanford's Summer High School program, where I teach a course in International Studies. One of the classes is on this very topic. Of course, I agreed to accept him. I sent Omar my answer in an email an hour ago."

"But he never responded," I murmur.

"No, not as of yet."

"Mr. Al-Salami, I'm so sorry to be the one to break the news to you, but Mr. Karman committed suicide this afternoon after losing his job."

He says nothing. "May he rest in peace," he whispers finally.

"I have to tell you that my son's paper was the issue behind his termination. You see, another parent took issue with the fact that it was forwarded from the school without the principal's permission. She used this misstep to lobby for Mr. Karman's resignation."

"Was that enough to get him fired?" Professor Al-Salami asks.

"That—and, in my opinion, her prejudice against him."

"I'm personally familiar with the issue of prejudice." The hardened edge in his voice makes me wince.

"As much as it pains me to say so, should that be reason enough to withdraw your offer to my son, I'd understand completely."

"If it were, her prejudice would win out, would it not?" he reasons. "To honor Omar's request, his friendship, and his life, the offer stands. I leave the decision in the hands of you and your son."

The pain in his voice breaks my heart.

～

I wait until Jack gets home, then we knock on Jeff's door together. At first, he doesn't answer. Finally, I hear a muffled, "What is it?"

"I think you'll want to hear what I have to say," I answer.

We hear his footsteps. The door creaks open, but Jeff backs away until he's up against the bed.

"Mr. Karman is dead. He committed suicide this afternoon."

Jeff staggers back onto his bed. "It's—it's because of my paper, isn't it?"

"No, Jeff. Your paper was the catalyst that small-minded people used as the excuse to get him fired. As it turns out, he was tired of the prejudice he encountered here, and he was concerned about the whereabouts of his family, who had fled terrorists in his birth country of Yemen."

The enormity of the news has Jeff stunned and shaking his head.

"I also want to tell you that I just got off the phone with Mr. Al-Salami."

"Emma found him? But, of course," Jeff says in answer to his own question.

"Mr. Al-Salami went to school with Mr. Karman. He's now a professor at Stanford. During the summer, he runs a two-week workshop for high school students who are interested in the area of International Studies. Mr. Karman had forwarded your paper in the hope that he'd accept you into the program, despite your age. After reading it, Professor Al-Salami agreed to do so. He was also impressed with it."

Jeff's eyes grow large. "Wow…" Suddenly, he frowns. "But I can't! I wouldn't feel right about it!"

"I thought you'd react that way, and I warned the professor it may be the case. He pointed out to me that the position is open, if you want it. He feels since your attendance was Mr. Karman's final request, he hopes you accept. That way, both of you can honor his memory."

"I don't know." Tears roll down Jeff's cheeks.

Jack sits down beside my son. "Jeff, prejudices are built on ignorance and fear. The more we learn, the greater chance we have of overcoming them. This isn't solely about Mr. Karman. It's also about you."

Jeff nods. He knows what Jack means: if Jeff is going to conquer the fear from the trauma of being held hostage, hearing it discussed openly and factually is a good start.

"Take the night to think about it. If you agree, I'm sure the professor will be glad to hear from you." I go to his desk and write down Professor Al-Salami's email and phone number.

We aren't out the door before Jeff picks up his cell phone. "Hello…is this Professor Al-Salami? My name is Jeff Stone…"

I have yet one more reason to be proud of my son.

14

Bare Roots

Besides seeds, seedlings, or potted in dirt, another way in which a plant might be sold is with "bare roots"—in other words, with all soil removed from its roots, so that the purchaser can more fully judge its healthiness. This method is predominant with trees, shrubs and perennials. Hint: The plumper and lighter the root, the healthier it is. It should bloom beautifully.

Just as it's easy to hide a sick plant in a pretty pot under lots of soil or peat moss, it's a cinch to mask a nasty disposition beneath a fake smile, false words, and a beautiful face. The root of a person's true character lies deep under the surface. Their actions are what casts light on who they truly are.

Judge your friends by that and your relationships will probably blossom for a lifetime.

THE NEXT MORNING, MARY AND I ARRIVE AT THE SCHOOL AN hour before classes. We head straight to the gym and knock on Coach Lonergan's door.

Mary's coach doesn't seem at all surprised to see us. She ushers us in. "Mary, I'd heard you'd called in sick yesterday. I presume it had something to do with your performance at the game."

Mary nods. "Coach Lonergan, it's not what you think."

Coach Lonergan holds up a hand. "Please don't apologize. I know the pressure you've been under since making the team. But I must admit, considering your determination and skill set during our practices, I was surprised and ultimately disappointed at your performance during the game." She hesitates, then adds, "Not everyone thrives in a competitive spotlight. If you feel the pressure is too great, I'll understand if you wish to resign from the team, and I won't stop you. However, if you're willing to give yourself a second chance, then by all means, I am too."

Mary sits straight up. Her coach's words of encouragement are all she needs to put her at ease and to put a smile back on her face. "Thank you, Coach, for believing in me. And yes, I'd be honored to continue on the team. However"—she takes a deep breath—"my actions at the game had nothing to do with anxiety, or illness, for that matter. Sara, Cara and Tara drugged my water bottle."

She places a thumb drive on the desk in front of Coach Lonergan. "This contains video evidence of the girls breaking into my locker and tampering with my water bottle. The second file is a report from a lab that analyzed the contents of the bottle. I was drugged with a roofie."

Coach Lonergan's eyes open wide.

"Coach, I know what you're thinking—that this will devastate the team—"

"You're wrong," Coach Lonergan interrupts her. "If anything, I'm thinking of the criminal charges they'll be facing—if you choose to prosecute them."

Mary thinks for a moment, "Really, I hadn't thought about that. I'm hoping that the shame of knowing what you and their parents will think of them will be enough."

"It won't. They'll also be kicked off the team—and I'm sure that once I make the principal aware of this, they'll be expelled from school, too." She shrugs. "A team is only as strong as its leaders. It's one of the reasons I'd hoped you'd stick it out with us."

"If that's the case, I'll accept your offer to keep me on the team." Mary stands up to shake her coach's hand.

Coach Lonergan stands up too—but hugs Mary instead. "I'm sorry you had to go through this. And I'm sure having to break the news to me wasn't easy."

Mary laughs. "I won't lie to you: I would have loved to have skipped the roofie, and gotten back a day of my life. Maybe someday I can laugh at seeing a video of me on the court. And, no, I don't take any joy in telling you what Sara and the others did to me. I only wish they didn't feel the need to hate me." She shrugs. "Then again, a wise person once told me, 'Every experience, even the tragic ones, are an opportunity to grow stronger.'"

And then Mary gives me a kiss.

THERE'S NOTHING MORE ENJOYABLE THAN A DAY IN WHICH THE only thing you do is exactly nothing.

Case in point: today, because there is no world crisis that needs my attention. And now that my daughter has dealt with her bullies, all family crises are taken care of as well.

Jack has a different way to unwind. By the time I get home, he has already mowed the front lawn. The way I see it, better him than me.

I sit on one of the chaises on the back terrace. My mind is busy planning tonight's dinner menu. We look forward to a quiet evening at home with the kids. I'll let Jack play chef and toss a few burgers on the grill. I'll make my patented potato salad, and I've got a killer recipe for kale salad.

In the meantime, I'll just sit here and do...*absolutely nothing.*

Until the phone rings.

The caller is Lori. "Donna, I'm in a panic! I've just had a call from the Daisy Scouts headquarters that the cookies are on a truck, to be delivered there, in Palm Springs! I'm in a bind. My oldest daughter has her ballet recital this afternoon. If we can't pick them up by three o'clock, we can't get them until Monday afternoon. Would you mind picking up our portion of the shipment?"

Yes, I would, but clearly, someone needs to help Lori. She

does so much for the Daisy Scouts already. So, I lie. "Sure, no problem."

"Thank you! You're a lifesaver! I'll text you the address now."

"Who was that?" Jack asks.

"Lori. She asked if I'd meet the troop's cookie delivery at the Daisy Scouts' headquarters—in Palm Springs, of all places."

"Would you like some company?" He grins at me. "I'll even let you drive the new Jackmobile."

I sigh my disappointment. "I'll take a rain check. The order is so large that we'll have to take the van. But sure, you can tag along."

Really, it was the grin that did it, but he doesn't need to know that.

And we're off.

WE'RE TOOLING UP I-405 WHEN ARNIE'S CALLER ID LIGHTS UP on my phone.

"If you're calling about the Daisy Scout cookies, don't worry. I'm on my way to pick them up now."

"So, you've heard from Ryan?"

"What? Now Ryan wants cookies, too? He always claims he's allergic to them."

"He's allergic to Daisy Scouts, not their cookies," Jack says. "I've caught him gobbling them up by the handful in Acme's break room."

"Donna, the corn delivery driver came clean with another drop of Exodus corn—or in this case, corn syrup, to DeeLiteFull Bakery, in Phoenix. They make custom cookies—specifically, for Daisy Scouts."

"Oh no," I murmur.

"Wellborne had an accomplice at the corn syrup processing plant. Dominic was sent to pick him up."

"He's home? Well, it's about damn time," I mutter. "I can't wait to see his lovely tan."

"At least Dominic got what we needed to track the deposit into Wellborne's account," Arnie informs us. "Unfortunately, it was a dead-end. The funds were issued by a private company in Hong Kong."

"Well, that certainly strengthens our suspicions that the MSS was involved," Jack replies.

"As for Wellborne's bakery accomplice, he's already squealing," Arnie continues. "Wellborne insisted the corn syrup was to be used in a specific batch of cookies: snickerdoodles. To confirm his accomplice's statement, Acme hacked into DeeLiteFull's security feed and production database. We have verification that the corn syrup was delivered, and that it was used as instructed. This cookie batch—along with other varieties—is now on a truck heading west on I-10, toward Palm Springs. From there, it will be sorted into the individual troops' shipments, and sent all over the country."

"Making it even harder to track the source," Jack reasons. "Is there any possibility that the corn syrup was used in the other cookies?"

Arnie sighs mournfully. "Let me put it this way—the

FDA doesn't want to take any chances." I'm sure he's thinking of his own sugar fix.

"Arnie, where is the truck now?" I ask.

"Satellite surveillance shows it's just east of the Arizona-California border."

"Got it. We'll do what we can to contain it. Alert the FDA, okay?"

"Already on it."

As you travel through the Los Angeles Metroplex, I-10 goes from being bumper-to-bumper (snaking through down-town), to stop-and-go (passing East Los Angeles), to flowing steadily (in and around Pomona), to practically empty (Thousand Palms).

When we're fifty miles east of Indio, heading toward California's border with Arizona, Arnie calls. "The driver has stopped to grab a bite to eat. It's a place called the Hot Wheels All-Nite Truck Stop. I'll send you the coordinates."

Jack laughs. "It's not necessary. I already know it. In fact, it's just fifteen minutes from where we are. The FDA can meet us back here. We'll call when we've secured the truck."

Jack knows of some all-night truck stop, in the middle of nowhere? *Interesting.* "One of your old hang-outs, I presume?" I ask.

"Not quite, but yes, I've been there. Do yourself a favor: pass on the cherry pie."

I'm sure there's a story in this. I'll have to pry it out of him one day with a piece of my own homemade cherry pie.

THE DEELITEFULL BAKERY TRUCK SITS BY ITSELF IN THE PARKING lot of the Hot Wheels All-Nite Truck Stop.

As instructed by Jack, I pull the car around to the back lot, but I keep the engine running.

The back door is closed. There's a tin bucket beside it labeled, SMOKERS LOUNGE.

Nice touch.

"Okay, here's the plan," he says. "I'll wait here while you drive back around to the front. Order a coffee, make goo-goo eyes with him, get cozy, grab his keys, and then tell him you've got to go to the little girl's room. I'll meet you here and you can hand them off to me. Then go back in and distract him until I leave with the truck."

"I may have a better idea. Just be standing by the truck, so that when I toss you the keys, you're ready to go." I reach for the door handle.

Jack grabs my hand to stop me. "Donna, if anything should happen—well, I'd like you to...what I'm trying to say is, will you—"

I put my fingers over his lips. "Jack, when will you learn not to ruin a perfectly good caper with your poorly timed romantic proposal?"

He feigns shock. "I thought any proposal was a good proposal."

"Men! You're all alike!" I kiss him—*hard*—on the mouth. When our lips part, I whisper, "Just keep trying."

And I'm out the door.

I ROAR BACK INTO THE FRONT PARKING LOT. THE DEELITEFULL'S delivery guy hears me, alright.

I pull up right below his window booth, so that he can watch as I purse my lips and apply an undercoat before running over them with a special custom lipstick—in this case, *Cherry Noir*. One smooch and it's beddy-bye time.

So that he gets the right idea, I blow him a kiss.

He's poised to chew a bacon strip, but he freezes. Finally, he rewards me with a grin. Considering how many of his teeth are missing, I wonder how long it will take for him to gum it down? I guess I'll find out if I stick around long enough to watch him do it.

This guy better not have stinky breath to go along with his rotted teeth.

As I suspected, the café is practically empty, except for lover boy, a potbellied cook, and a bucktoothed waitress scratching her head over a Mad Libs Sudoku flip book. Delivery dude is gaunt, tatted, and eager to make my acquaintance. The truck's keys are on the table, next to his plate of bacon and eggs.

"Is this seat taken?" I point to his side of the booth. By the way I ask, you'd think it was rush hour at Grand Central Station.

"Only if you're buying," he chortles.

I ease down beside him. "Depends on what you're selling," I giggle. I signal the waitress.

She sighs heavily. Gee, I hope I'm not stealing her boyfriend.

By the time she saunters over, I've made up my mind what I want: outta here.

Instead, I order an egg over easy, bacon, and a cuppa. That should keep both her and the cook busy while I flirt with my new beau.

"You've got quite an appetite." His unibrow rises to his monk's cut.

"If only you knew," I say coyly.

He's not only eating his eggs; he's wearing them, too—on his upper lip. I reach across him for the paper napkin dispenser. Oops, I graze his forearm with my breast. It doesn't seem to perturb him.

At least, not above his waist.

With napkin in hand, I wipe off his egg mustache. Yep, that's got his attention.

We lock eyes.

The next thing he knows, we're locking lips, too.

It'll be the last thing he'll remember before dozing off.

I leave him face down in his bacon and eggs, pocketing the keys as I go.

The waitress is too busy to notice him, or me, heading for the front door.

～

I TRAIL JACK IN THE TRUCK TO THE INDIO TOWN LIMITS. As promised, FDA agents are waiting for us.

Jack tosses them the keys to the DeeLiteFull truck, and jumps in my van. Instinctively, he reaches over to kiss me—

Before I can stop him.

The whole way back, Jack sleeps like a baby.

BY THE TIME WE HIT ORANGE COUNTY, HE'S AWAKE AND refreshed.

"Did I nod off?" he asks.

"Yes," I reply. "And as your penance, you have to go with me to Hilldale Elementary to break the news to the Daisies that they won't be selling cookies this year."

"They'll never know what a better choice that was than the alternative."

I'm just happy that we avoided a disaster that would have haunted our children for the rest of their lives, had they survived it.

TRISHA AND AUNT PHYLLIS WAVE AT US WE PULL UP IN FRONT of Hilldale Elementary School. They aren't alone. The whole Daisy Scout troop is present, accounted for, and raring to go on their cookie deliveries.

The first to get her order fulfilled is the school's principal, Miss Darling. As a former scout herself, having a successful troop was one of her stated goals upon joining the school. She stands front and center with the mother who made it all possible: Lori.

"Yikes. This should be awkward," Jack murmurs.

Suddenly, an idea comes to me. "Let me handle this."

Jack laughs. "Gladly."

I've barely parked my car when everyone runs over. In no time, my SUV is surrounded.

The color leaves Jack's face. "I've seen when mobs get angry. Maybe we should just skedaddle."

"Chicken," I tease. Frankly, I'm just as frightened. For all I know, what I have to say may get us tarred and feathered, but it's worth a try.

Some of the girls have their noses pressed against the SUV's window. But their faces fall when they realize there's nothing in the car.

"Where are all the cookies?" one girl shouts.

She's not the only one who's noticed either. The crowd's concern starts as a murmur, but crescendos into a wail of panic.

I jump out of the car and hold up my hands to silence them. "I'm sorry, but I've got some very bad news. The truck carrying the shipment of cookies bound for Los Angeles met with an accident. All the cookies were destroyed. I'm so sorry; we won't be getting any this year."

The crowd's disappointment is shouted in unison. In no time at all it's joined by the scouts' sobs.

"Why—this is awful!" Lori exclaims. "If we have to return the purchasers' money, the troop will go bankrupt!"

"All the troops in the area are facing the same problem. However"—I take a deep breath—"I think I have a solution, if we're all willing to pitch in."

"What is it?" one anxious mother asks.

"We make the cookies ourselves—with the help of our Daisy Scouts."

My suggestion is met with silence.

"It'll be fun, and a great experience in teamwork," I insist. "Isn't that what Daisy Scouts is all about?" Again, not a peep. But, no one's hung a noose over the school's flagpole either, so I push ahead. "Each of us has a favorite cookie recipe. Many are similar to our customers' favorites. To top it off, nothing is better than a homemade cookie! Am I right?"

A murmur goes through the crowd. I strain my ears for the word "lynching," and am relieved to hear, "possible" instead.

"Are we supposed to tie up our kitchens for the whole night?" asks one mother. "I can't do that!"

"And what about the ingredients? Who pays for that?" another chimes in.

"The cost may chip away at our profit, but it'll still be healthy enough to fund all of this year's projects," Lori assures the others.

"As for the kitchen, I've got a suggestion," Miss Darling pronounces. "Why not use the school cafeteria's kitchen? As for ingredients, as soon as you write down your recipes, Lori and Donna can coordinate a list and send a couple of runners with vans over to Costco."

"We'll coordinate an assembly line of mixers, bakers, and

packagers," Lori adds. "For packaging, instead of bags, we can use cellophane tied with ribbon."

"We can even tag the orders with notes. I'm a lousy baker, but I'm a professional calligrapher, so I'll offer to write them."

I grin. "You're hired."

A mother shrugs. "I've got a killer chocolate mint cookie recipe. It's better than the Daisy version, if I do say so myself."

I pull a notebook from the van. "Write it down here. I've got something I call a Donna Doodle. It's similar to a snickerdoodle, but a different combination of spices. It tastes something like pumpkin pie."

"Yum," murmurs a mother. "I'd buy that."

"Great idea! Why don't we can put together a cookie recipe book, and sell it online?" Lori suggests.

Soon, everyone has bought into my Plan B.

Twenty minutes later, we've matched recipes to our orders.

It'll be a long night, but from the look of excitement on our daughters' faces, I know it will be memorable too.

By midnight, the last cookie is wrapped, and ready to go.

Like the rest of the scouts, Trisha nodded off around ten. The girls slept on workout mats in a corner of the cafeteria, while their parents boxed their own orders. Then after checking it twice, they loaded their cookies and sleepy children into their cars and went home.

Miss Darling walks Lori and me to the door. "I'll supervise the moms who've offered to stay behind for cleanup. Go home and get some sleep."

Lori pulls us into a group hug. "I can't believe how generous everyone was with their time!"

Miss Darling pats her hand. "Sometimes, it takes a crisis for others to realize what is at stake, and to chip in. If it's your child's happiness, you'll do what you can to be her hero."

From the proud smiles on every parents' face tonight, I'd say this troop has a new annual tradition.

THE NEXT MORNING, I TEXT TRISHA'S CUSTOMERS THAT THEIR orders are ready for pick-up or delivery, along with rave reviews by last night's samplers: the girls themselves.

When Arnie reads that his cookie order is homemade, he's too excited to wait for me to drop it off at Acme later this afternoon. In order to take the whole order in one trip, he shows up at the house with Abu's ice cream truck. Abu has tagged along, to help him load it up.

Jeff and Evan sit side by side at the kitchen table, teaching Trisha how to reconcile sales and the deliveries being made later by Jack and Aunt Phyllis. Scanning their spreadsheets, Abu whistles softly. "Wow! These sales numbers are phenomenal—not to mention the reviews!"

He can't help himself. He picks one of the Donna Doodles off a plate in the center of the table and takes a bite.

"I can see why they get such raves," he declares. Suddenly, there's a gleam in his eye. "Donna, I've been thinking about the pie shop. Why don't we add cookies as a different product line?"

"Sure, okay. But, Abu, if we're successful, are you going to quit Acme and become a franchise mogul?"

His laugh comes out as a snort. For a fleeting moment, his eyes widen at the thought of what could be his final endgame. But then, he sobers up. "As tempting as that is, you and I both know we'd be bored working behind a bakery counter."

I laugh. "Who said anything about me? I've already made my choice."

"I guess I have too," Abu says softly.

I give him a hug. "Good, because I would have missed you."

He shrugs. "Once in the game, always in the game." He waves as he goes out the back door. The tinkling melody of *The Farmer in the Dell* can be heard as his ice cream truck makes its way down the block.

Evan stops his tallying and clears his throat. "Donna, I've made a decision, too—about my mom."

"Okay." I brace myself for the worst.

"I know how badly you want me to say yes, and I wish in my heart that I could forgive her. At this point in my life, I can't." Tears glaze his eyes. "Still, I know that it's not just my feelings that have to be considered. She has something Acme needs, so I will agree to go, if only for that. But—well, don't expect me to like it."

"I don't, Evan. On Acme's behalf, I want to thank you for your decision." In the hope of making our visit seem less formidable, I add, "Jack is joining us. Arnie may, too." It is Ryan's idea—not necessarily to intimidate Catherine, but in case accessing her intel needs onsite technical support, or for that matter, more muscle.

Evan shrugs at this news. For him, nothing will turn this into a joyride.

As for Catherine, if she's expecting a happy birthday, she'll be sadly disappointed.

Learning how badly your child hates you is the worst gift ever.

———————————————————

15

Forcing

———————————————————

The process for hastening a plant's growth to maturity or bloom is called forcing.

Can a person also be forced to grow beyond their years? All too often, fate provides a catalyst. Dealing with starvation, living in a war zone, or witnessing the death of a loved one are all examples of this.

Whereas forcing a flower into bloom may make for a beautiful garden, should life step in to propel a child beyond his innocence, you can only pray it will make him stronger.

There are enough fucked up people in the world as it is.

THE FEDERAL PRISON CAMP IN ALDERSON, WEST VIRGINIA HAS a gate, but no guard station. It hugs the banks of the Greenbrier River in a verdant valley surrounded by low rolling hills that slope up to a thick-leafed national forest. There is no fence surrounding its one-hundred and fifty-nine acres, just an intermittent red-tip hedge. The classic Georgian buildings scattered throughout leave the impression that one is on the campus of an elite private college.

Evan must think so too, because he doesn't realize we're within spitting distance of his mother's current home until I warn him, "We're here."

I watch through the rear-view mirror as he slumps down even further in the back seat. He says nothing. His face reflects no concern for his mother's circumstances, just unfathomable sadness.

Arnie has come with us after all. I'm glad, if only because his constant chatter about Star Wars trivia, online gaming tricks, and his hacking exploits kept the flight—not to mention the short trip from the airport—from being silent. The few words Evan mumbled were directed at George, who encouraged him to sit up in the cockpit.

In other words, it's painfully obvious that Evan resents me for my role in making him face his mother, even if he hasn't come out and said so.

Jack is riding shotgun. He stares out the window, but by the way he squeezes my hand, I presume he actually saw Evan's reaction in the side view mirror and knows how much it hurts me, especially since I can't stand her either.

Few bushes or trees line the seemingly endless driveway that curves around the minimum-security prison camp. In other words, even if you get a hankering to break out, there are few places to hide. When compared to some of the other women's prisons around the country, odds are you'll stay put, and no one would blame you. Alderson could pass for a country club. The rules are reasonable, the duties are light, and on the cruelty scale, the guards are a step above the worst nun in a Catholic reformatory for wayward girls.

We park outside the main building. It seems as if we take a collective deep breath before exiting the car. When we enter the lobby, the female guard who stands behind the glass cubicle that serves as a reception desk checks her list to verify that, yes, we're on the guest roster. She then scrutinizes our drivers' licenses.

"Not you." She points at Jack. "Or you." She motions to Arnie.

"Why not?" Frantically, Evan's eyes shift from the guard to Jack.

"They ain't on the list. Just you"—she points at Evan —"and her." She points at me.

Jack puts his hand on Evan's shoulder. "You can do this."

It takes a moment for Evan's breathing to get back to normal. When he gives me the high sign, I nod at the guard.

She buzzes us into a narrow hallway that leads to several glass-walled visiting rooms.

WE STOP IN THE DOORWAY OF THE ONE HOLDING CATHERINE. Two guards are sitting at the farthest side of the room. When we enter, they glance up from their backgammon game, then exchange shrugs. One is a slight, petite woman with a curly blond ponytail under her cap. Her nails are long, and painted turquoise, with a diamond embedded in the middle fingers. The other is a beefy man whose legs are too thick and long to slip under the small table.

Neither have firearms, but both have stun guns clipped to their belts.

Catherine stands tall, her head held high. She faces the window. But then, as if sensing us, she turns around.

Evan's eyes grow small as he scrutinizes her for the first time in almost a year. I saw her just a couple of months ago, and even since then there is a marked difference in her. Her khaki prisoner's uniform now hangs loosely. Her face is gaunt to the point that there are now hollows in her cheeks. Black shadows haunt her eyes. Lips that were once frozen in a perpetual smirk are now pursed into a tight fretful line.

She looks ill. Then again, if my children refused to see me, I'd worry myself sick too.

When Catherine sees her son, the frenzy in her eyes dampens with tears of hope—

—Whereas Evan's glare is a rock-solid wall of contempt.

Realizing this, her lids drop low, like a scrim of resignation. Nonetheless, her simple declaration—"You came"—is etched in hope.

"What choice did I have?" Evan isn't posing a question as much as he's letting her know where she stands with him: nowhere.

"You've grown into your father." She makes it sound like a death sentence.

Evan's hearty laugh shows that he thinks otherwise. "That's the nicest thing you've ever said to me, Mother."

She flinches, as if dodging the barb that has backfired on her. "The very least you can do is wish me a happy birthday," she mutters.

Instead, he gives her a shrug. "I'm here. Isn't that enough?"

"Have you lost all love for me?" The question is barely audible.

"It died with the knowledge of what you did to my father." His tone is so devoid of feeling that he could have been commenting on the weather, as opposed to the death that tore his family apart.

"Then, why are you here?"

He shrugs. "You summoned me, remember?"

She acknowledges his declaration with a grimace, but the way her eyes sweep over him is proof that she has yet to give up on him; she cannot yet acknowledge his abandonment of her.

"And you made a promise to Donna." His declaration gives her a new target:

Me.

Her stare flares with anger, then smolders with renewed hatred. "I lied." She starts for the door.

Evan grabs her by the wrist. "Tell them what they need to know—*or I'll never come back.*"

The hope that he means what he says—that she'll see him again—extinguishes her contempt, for now, anyway. She signals me closer with a nod.

I glance over at the guards. The female one looks over. Her eyes narrow into a curious stare, but the murmur of "Gammon," from her competitor, forces her to look down again. She expresses her wariness with a frown.

Evan reads my cue. "Hey, wow, dude! You see this better move, right?" He walks over to the male guard and points to a disk on the board.

"Talk fast," I mutter to Catherine.

Nervously, she twists her wedding ring, an antique with a diamond. "Your ex had something on Lee. And now I have it."

"I presume you're talking about the accidental death involving the woman Lee loved. It's old news."

Catherine snorts loud enough that the female guard looks over suspiciously. "Murder? That's nothing compared to this!"

To call her bluff, I ask, "Why would Carl have trusted you with it?"

"Because he wanted to ensure Lee would toe the line, as per our agreement—his, Lee's and mine." She leans back in her chair. "You know Carl—always the consummate puppet master."

Just then the male guard chortles, "Yo, Tori! Pay attention. You're making this too easy for me."

I look up to see the female guard staring at me. When our eyes meet, she gives me the finger. What a psycho. I never thought I'd run into someone who made Catherine seem normal by comparison.

Finally, I break our staring contest to murmur, "I'm waiting with bated breath, Catherine."

"Three words." She leans in closer. *"Follow the money."*

"Next you'll be telling me that greed is good. You'll have to do better than quote classic movie lines in order to get an early release from POTUS."

Catherine quits twisting her ring, if only to grab my hand and hiss, "Don't be such a moron, Donna. Trust me, the moment Lee learns what I have, the Quorum will too—and I'll be dead! I'm giving Acme what it needs to—"

"What?" I can't believe my ears. "Do you have proof that Lee is part of the Quorum?"

I don't realize that Tori is standing behind me until she sneers, "You two have gotten real cozy."

"Don't worry, newbie," Catherine assures her. "You're still my favorite."

Tori frowns. "You'll have plenty of time to prove it. The party's over."

"Bullshit!" Catherine counters. "You heard the warden! I was supposed to have half an hour with my son!"

"You blew it when you handed your girlfriend that piece of paper." Tori grabs my fist and pries open my fingers.

We're staring down at a tiny piece of paper. "But…where did that come from?"

Catherine glares at me. "What is this, a set-up?" Angrily, she rises to her feet.

"Are you immediate family?"

Without thinking, I shake my head.

"I thought so!" Tori growls as she turns to Catherine. "You're trying to smuggle contraband out of the building!"

The next thing I know, Tori slams Catherine's head onto the table.

Stunned, Catherine slumps to the floor.

By the way the male guard bolts out of his seat, even he is thrown off by Tori's actions.

Evan isn't far behind him. For the first time, he's concerned for his mother. When he kneels beside her, she grasps his hand with both of hers, as if it's a lifeline. "I'm… so sorry," she finally rasps.

Catherine flinches and yelps as Tori lifts her from under her shoulders. "What the hell did you poke me with—a needle?" Catherine bellows.

Instead of answering her, the guard wrenches her arm behind her back, "Now, say goodbye to all the nice people," she sneers.

As Catherine passes me, her eyes are wide with fear. Still, she has the courage to shout, "You've now got what you need! Remember—you promised."

This gives Tori the only excuse she needs to goose-step her prisoner out the door.

"Jesus, Tori, lighten up! This ain't Rikers!" the other guard calls after them, then sighs. Turning back toward us, he mumbles, "No problem, folks. The worst that can happen is Lady Catherine will be barred from tonight's Bingo game." He jogs after them.

Jack must have heard the commotion because he's now

running down the hall. When he reaches me, he asks, "Is it true what the guard said? Did she pass you anything?"

"No, I swear it!"

He shakes his head. "Then where did the paper come from?"

I shrug. "I think Catherine is right. It was a fix, and it had to be perpetrated by the female guard, Tori."

"Something's wrong here," Jack mutters. "We should follow them."

I grab Evan's arm. "Let's do it."

"No," Evan insists. "It's not that I don't believe you, Donna. It's just that—well, I know my mother. For some reason, she's pushed that woman's buttons. It had nothing to do with us."

He may be right, but my spider senses are tingling. If he's wrong and Catherine is in danger, how will we get proof of her claim?

Jack looks from Evan to me. I shrug. "Evan did us a solid. It's his call."

Evan shivers. "Let's get out of here."

He's the first out the door. I'm on his heels.

Evan has already climbed into the back seat when he realizes his fisted hand is holding something. It's his mother's ring—the one she twisted so nervously. He stares down at it for the longest time, then hands it to me.

Needless to say, this surprises me. "Don't you want to hold onto it for her?"

He shakes his head. "Why should I? You'll see her before I do."

"But, you told her that you'd come back."

"I lied," he says calmly. "I guess what they say is right. The apple doesn't fall far from the tree."

It's on the tip of my tongue to tell him that he's made from stronger stuff; his roots are deep in the DNA of his father, Robert—who was one of the most honest and loving men I ever knew.

Instead, I keep my mouth shut and pocket the ring, for safekeeping.

Someday, he'll want it back.

JACK DRIVES US BACK TO GREENBRIER VALLEY AIRPORT, WHERE George has the jet fueled up and ready to take us home.

We've just driven onto the tarmac and boarded Acme's plane when Evan's cell phone rings. "It's the prison. I guess Mother coerced the guards into giving her back her calling privileges." Still, he can't bring himself to answer it.

"Take it," Jack insists.

Evan winces, but does as he is told. A concerned look rises on his face. "Who...*what? ...Dead?* But how could that be? I just saw her!"

Jack takes the phone and pushes the speaker button. A second later, we hear the warden's voice: "—cardiac arrhythmia. We've done everything we can. The doctor pronounced her dead just two minutes ago. We'll be doing an autopsy as soon as possible. It should take a couple of hours. But, since you're in town, I presume you'll want to claim the body immediately afterward."

Evan collapses into a seat.

I put my arms around him. Jack takes the phone off speaker and moves away in order to answer the warden's questions.

As it turns out, Catherine will be leaving with us after all.

Sobbing, Evan mutters, "I was so cruel! I wanted her to know how much I hated her."

"But you didn't hate her, did you?" Arnie asks.

Evan shakes his head. His "no" comes out of him as a long, mournful moan.

I release my hold on Evan, but not until after I give him a kiss on the forehead.

Just as I do this, I notice a limousine pulling up to another private jet on the tarmac—a Gulfstream 650ER, just like Acme's plane. The driver hops out and looks at the airstairs. Since no one is there, he walks back to the car.

The tinted back window slides down. A hand taps impatiently on the sill.

The nails are long, and turquoise—with diamond studs on the middle fingers.

It has to be Tori.

But the woman who leans forward to talk to the driver isn't blond. Her hair is long and dark. She takes off her sunglasses in order to give him the stink eye as if it's his fault that no one is manning her getaway vehicle.

That's when I realize she is Asian.

More to the point, I recognize her as Liang Xia.

I nudge Jack. "Look over there! It's Xia!"

All heads swivel in her direction. We watch as the limo driver shrugs his shoulders in resignation.

Xia glances down at her watch and angrily shakes her head.

"What the hell?" Jack murmurs. "I'd say this is a small world, but I presume it's more than a coincidence."

"I'll say," I assure him. "She was posing as Catherine's prison guard!"

Evan does a double take. "But...the guard was blond. And she didn't have Asian features."

"Xia is a master of disguises," I assure him.

"Are you saying that she may have had something to do with Catherine's death?" Arnie asks.

"I'm sure of it. Xia cut her off before she could finish telling me the intel she felt would get her out of there." I turn to Jack. "Xia has been shadowing us since we discovered the existence of the bad seeds. Maybe what Catherine knew is in some way tied to it as well. We can't just let her waltz away!"

"Her pilot is inside, filing his flight plan to Hong Kong, from what he told me. He was waiting in line behind me," George explains. "In fact, the whole crew—the co-pilot and the flight attendant were in there too, grabbing a bite to eat. She must have arrived earlier than they expected."

I frown. "So, she's finally leaving the country."

"Maybe not." Jack smiles. "It's a charter, so chances are she hasn't met her pilot yet—or George and me, for that matter. So, why don't we take her on a detour?"

"You mean, put her on *this* plane? That's brilliant!" Then it hits me—we can't put Evan in the middle of all of this. "But"—I nod toward Evan. "We have to stay put."

"No, you don't," Evan declares.

We all turn to him. His face is damp, but his eyes are cold with determination. "Donna, if this woman killed my mother, you can't let her get away! Arnie and I will stay here until it's time to"—he takes a deep breath—"get my mother. In the meantime, we'll make the necessary arrangements to bring Mother home with us…to California."

Where she and his dad grew up. And now it's his home too.

Jack puts his hand on the boy's shoulder. "Then, we'd better get moving." He nods to George. "Don't you keep an extra uniform here, on the plane?"

"Yep, along with a tie, hat, and shirt—the whole nine yards," George says. "It's in the closet next to the cockpit."

"Great. I'll change into it, but I'm doing without the jacket and hat. I'm your new flight attendant." Jack turns to Arnie. "How quickly can you hack the limo driver's cell phone?"

"I'll have it done before you put on George's tie." He's got his laptop open in no time flat, and is clicking away on the keyboard. Arnie's computer is equipped with UFED software—in other words, it also acts as a universal forensic extracting device.

Well, what do you know? Jack is just tucking his shirt into the uniform's gabardine slacks when Arnie declares, "Done."

Jack gives him a thumbs-up. "Great. You and Evan get back into the car, and pull it close to the terminal. After you park, call the driver as if you're me, ask him where he is, and tell him that he's in front of the wrong equipment." Jack turns to me. "George will greet Xia at the bottom of the airstairs. When she comes onboard, I'll introduce myself and show her a couple of its unique features—the sleeping cabin and deluxe bath suite. Donna, until she's tucked in and we're airborne, you can hide in the cockpit."

I frown at the term "tucked in," only because now I know Xia too well.

But I know Jack even better. He's only got eyes for me.

16

Deadheading

The act of pinching or cutting off spent flowers.

This is an airline term as well. When airline personnel are dead-heading, they are hitching a ride on a plane after their shifts have ended.

Usually, if available, and they are a pilot, they are given a seat in the cockpit. If they're unlucky, it'll be in Economy (a.k.a., the slave galley). If they're very lucky, they'll get one of the luxury seats in the first-class cabin.

No one is ever tied to the wing or the tail, even if the distance is short, and the altitude is low. However, if you feel it will get you the intel you need, try it with your prisoner during your next extraordinary rendition. No one will stop you.

Not to mention, waterboarding is so last year.

By the time Xia's limo has pulled up to Acme's plane, I'm in the cockpit with the door closed. From there, I can watch everyone else via the mini-cam feeds that cover both the interior and exterior of the plane, as seen through the cockpit's overhead monitor.

George stands at the airstairs. He smiles and waves as the driver stops the car, and joins the man as he opens the trunk to retrieve Xia's luggage. As George holds on to her suitcase, the driver opens the back door in order to help Xia out of the car.

Seeing this, George removes his captain's cap, placing it under his left arm in deference to his new client. After shaking her hand, he escorts her up the steps.

Jack greets Xia at the door with a smile and once-over gaze. When he holds out his hand, she moves so close that she's standing breast-to-chest with him. Granted, private jets are small, but this is one of the larger ones, so there's no need for her to get so cozy, unless she's looking for a hottie like Jack to ride her even higher than the requisite mile.

And does Jack know it. The proof is in the way in which his dimpled grin dazzles, and how he times his smoldering gaze just as he murmurs the phrase, "If you get lonely, I'll take you on a tour of the *cockpit*."

Instinctively, any female within one hundred yards of a handsome man will flirt, and all that implies. Xia is within five centimeters of him. She smirks and simpers, and tosses her hair. She's on a high, and it's not just the pheromones wafting between them.

Most exterminators look to let off steam after a hit. No doubt about it, Jack is catnip to a woman like Xia who is just off a mission and has twelve or so hours to kill as she deadheads back to her home base. I know what she's thinking, because I'd be thinking it too: why not do so while lying in the strong, muscular arms of some ready, willing, and able boy-toy, whose one job is to make your journey as pleasurable as possible?

Finally, Jack excuses himself, but not before he personally snaps her into her seatbelt. Yes, his hand brushes her thigh as he tightens the belt around her hips. And in case she still doesn't get the message, he leans in close when he hands her a sleep mask.

"Once we're airborne, I'll be able to take care of any and all your needs," he promises her. "So, don't worry, you'll have plenty of time to relax."

Ha! He certainly knows his way around a double-entendre.

"I plan on doing a lot more than sleeping." Her tone is naughty. She nods toward the back of the plane, where the bath suite is located. "After takeoff, I'm taking a nice, warm shower. It'll be nice to have someone to scrub my back."

Hmmm, not a bad idea. And I know just what I can use to do it.

JACK JOINS US IN THE COCKPIT. AS I GET UP FROM THE CO-PILOT position in order to move into the jump seat behind it, I make sure to rub against him. "Tight squeeze, wouldn't you say?" I ask him in a breathy little-girl whisper.

His response is a hard, long kiss. When we come up for air, he murmurs, "That's yet another reason to make an honest man of me. I'll have to quit flirting with honeypots."

I sigh. "That has got to be the least romantic proposal yet. And you keep wondering why I turn you down."

"You're tempting fate," he warns me. "I may not be around forever."

"I'll take my chances. We're doing this right, or not at all."

"Folks, we've been cleared for takeoff," George reminds us. "Let's get this show on the road."

Wheels-up is bumpy. Apparently, a big storm is blowing in from the west. But as soon as we break through the cloud cover and into stark blue stratosphere, George levels off at the maximum cruising altitude: fifty-one thousand feet.

Xia unbuckles and heads for the sleeping cabin. She's in there just long enough to open her suitcase and pull out a white silk robe and a toiletries case, which she takes with her into the plane's luxury spa bathroom.

How convenient, Xia has left the bathroom door open. There is no doubt in her mind that Jack will take her up on her offer.

"I hope she doesn't mind a party crasher," I mutter.

He shrugs. "I presumed you'd want to do the honors. But

remember, Donna"—he taps the monitor—"I'm watching, so play nice."

I frown. "Are you kidding? After what she did to Catherine—*to Evan*?"

"You really don't want to kill her. Otherwise, we'll never have the verification we need that China was behind the killer seeds, let alone Catherine's death."

He's got a point. But after I drag her into Acme's Club Dread and she squeals her guts out, all bets are off.

I WAIT UNTIL I HEAR THE WATER RUNNING AND THE SOUND OF the shower door closing, then I walk soundlessly toward the bedroom.

Quickly, I rummage through her suitcase. Jesus, she's got enough sex toys in a zip pouch to open her own boutique— mostly dildos, but also a few nipple clamps, a ball gag, an interesting cock ring that looks like an adjustable lasso, and another that looks like a hard plastic gear. I pocket the lasso and gear ring, along with some pink fuzzy cuffs, nipple clamps, and the ball gag. I won't be using them in the tradi-tional way, but when you travel without a gun, you have to be creative.

Some of the items still have their price tags, so I guess she hasn't been too lucky on this mission. Or maybe I've kept her too busy. No wonder she's salivating after Jack.

She must have ditched the guard's uniform, but she kept

the one thing I suspect she used to kill Catherine: a bottle of liquid Digitalis. Next to it are a couple of syringes.

After filling one of them and capping the needle, I head toward the bathroom.

THE LARGE HIGH-POWER RAIN SHOWERHEAD IS CAUSING SUCH A deluge that Xia's slim body is a mere shadow, engulfed in its hot mist.

Shampooing her hair, she has her back to me. As she works her fingers through the suds and wet tendrils, I think of Catherine. I may not have liked my former friend, but I owe her this much.

Let me just say that Xia's off-key attempt at Taylor Swift's *Shake it Off* would earn her a gong in a WeHo karaoke bar. My own way of shutting her up is to slip the lasso around her neck and jerk it tightly, so that it's now a noose.

She chokes through the realization that she's not alone. Instinctively, she reaches up with her hands to loosen my grip, but she's too late. By then, I've slammed her head against one side of the marble shower stall, then the other.

When I pull her out of the tub, she's spewing water. Finally, she lets loose with a litany of curses in Mandarin. I recognize *qù sǐ* (go to hell) and *byao zhi yang duh* (son of a bitch) before she moves on to a few choice gender-specific insults. I take it personally when she calls me a *cho san ba* (bitch).

Words should never hurt me. That being said, sticks,

stones, and a well-positioned punch will break her bones, which is why I stick my index and middle fingers through the gear-spoke cock ring before making a fist and slamming it into her face.

It stuns her enough that when she comes to, I've got her on her knees, in front of the toilet.

She shivers, but knows better than to talk smack this time.

"That's better," I tell her. "Time for a little heart-to-heart, Xia."

She opts for the silent treatment—that is, until I plunge her face into the toilet.

When I lift her head, she snorts like a porpoise.

I brush off the few wayward droplets from my blouse. "Let's try this again. When you were in San Francisco, you handed your colleague, the MSS operative Yang Cheng, four postcards validating that the killer seeds were in the process of being distributed to farms throughout the United States."

Xia's eyes narrow in anger. "You intercepted Cheng and decoded the cards?"

I nod.

"You idiot! But I presume the seeds have already been distributed!"

"Thankfully, no. We were able to track them down—or the products made from them—before they reached the public."

"Thank goodness." She truly seems relieved.

"Wait...you mean, you didn't want the seeds to get out

there? But we thought it was an act of bioterrorism by your government!"

"You must have played hooky during Geography class, *sha bi*," she mutters.

Translation: stupid cunt.

I sigh. "Your taunt rolls off me, like water off a duck's back. Speaking of water—"

Once again, I plunge her face into the toilet. Here's hoping this baptism loosens her tongue.

When I pull her up, she's gagging.

"Do you want to try again to explain why I should believe your claim that the Chinese aren't involved?" I ask.

"Because, my dear Mrs. Stone, it doesn't make sense! Considering that your country is practically China's supermarket, why the hell would we do such a thing? My country imports close to a million and a half metric tons of corn from the United States, not to mention tons of specialty items and novelty foods containing corn"—Xia glances down at my backside—"which is why we're getting as fat as you Americans. And besides, my family—my parents, my children— live in China! The last thing I'd want is for them to die."

"If this act of bioterrorism wasn't initiated by the Chinese, who created and distributed the killer seeds?"

"You are such a fool." She taunts by clicking her tongue at me. "It was the Quorum."

"How do you know this?"

"I guess you never got the memo. I've been freelance for at least two years now. The Quorum is my biggest client. Your dearly departed ex, Carl, certainly knew how to make it worth my while." She smiles knowingly. "Fringe benefits. Got to love them."

Interesting. *Still, if she knew Carl like I knew Carl...Oh... Oh...Oh, what a jerk.* "And you tried to double-cross the Quorum by leaking their plan to the Chinese?"

"I had nowhere else to go! Maybe Putin, eh? You and I both know that Russia would have loved watching its two largest enemies face off over some misinformation. Little does it know that the Quorum is also working on a fatal microbe that thrives in caviar—but I digress." She rolls her eyes.

To get her on track, I ask, "Why did you kill Dr. Wellborne's file clerk, Jilly McIntosh?"

"I didn't, you idiot! *He* did. Jilly confronted that odious man. She told him she was turning him into Homeland Security, for treason. He killed her in the file room." Xia smiles. "Little did he know she'd planted a webcam on a shelf. It caught him in the act, then he buried her body who knows where."

Sadly, I know.

"He didn't know if he covered his tracks well enough, and was panicking. The Quorum sent me into SeedPlenish undercover, to find out why Wellborne was late with the second shipment of Exodus seeds. When I found out exactly what the seeds were meant to do, I had to stop it."

"To tell you the truth, Xia, it's still a toss-up as to whether I believe you. Where is the proof—the webcam video?"

She smirks. "A link to it is on one of the cards I handed

off to Yang Cheng. Ha! I guess your ComInt people are too stupid to break the cipher." She shrugs.

It must be contained in the last postcard still to be decoded. Well, breaking three out of four ciphers in less than seventy-two hours wasn't too bad.

"It's also uploaded in a secure cloud," Xia adds. "When you work for the Quorum, it's always nice to have these little insurance policies."

I wonder how many juicy little tidbits Carl had on his Quorum associates. I guess now we'll never find out.

"I presume the Quorum has no idea that you leaked their plan," I say.

Xia's eyes narrow in anger. "It doesn't. And it won't, if I can help it." She attempts a smirk. "By the way, Mrs. Stone, you have no reason to be so smug about your own country's reaction to this scheme. As it turns out, the Quorum approached the United States' Secretary of Agriculture. Even after witnessing a demonstration, Howard Harkness practically laughed in the Quorum envoys' faces. He claimed that the Quorum's threats were hollow."

"And I presume the Quorum felt that a pandemic would convince him otherwise, which is why the seeds were released in the first place," I reason.

"Correct. And in anticipation of the panic that would ensue, the Quorum has been buying up the corn commodities market in other countries, through Chinese brokers. That way, the Chinese take the fall for an act of terrorism on U.S. soil, giving your politicians the perfect opportunity to ramp up the arms race." She shrugs. "It would have been a big fat payday for everyone: your political hacks and their cozy bedfellows, and of course, the defense contractors. As for the Quorum, it would have made two killings: in international corn futures, and in munitions sales. To cover his ass, Secretary Harkness' plan was to disavow any previous knowledge of the plan. As for your president, had you not stopped the distribution of the Exodus strain, he would lie to the public, expressing full confidence in the ability to recall the Exodus seeds and food. And if the Administration failed to do so, it would downplay the extent of any subsequent pandemic."

I'd be willing to bet that Secretary Harkness never told Lee about his meeting with the Quorum. "If President Chiffray had known—"

A smirk curls on Xia's lips. "What makes you think he didn't?"

"I don't believe you!"

She laughs. "I couldn't care less."

I'd love to wipe that smile off her face, and the toilet bowl is certainly hard enough to break her teeth. But if she can't talk, she can't give us the answers we need.

Like the one foremost on my mind: "Xia, why did you kill Catherine?"

"You're not going to like what I have to say," she warns me.

"I'm disgusted by everything you've told me. At this point, you have nothing to lose."

"I was sent by Lee Chiffray, okay?" Noting the disappointed look on my face, she shrugs. "Sorry to burst your bubble, but in all honesty, you shouldn't be crushing on such a powerful man, darling. He's got too many others to choose from."

"For your information, Xia, I'm a one-man woman. And, let's be honest. If you were actually getting a little POTUS action—or any action at all—there wouldn't be so many price tags on your play toys." I hold up the gear-shaped cock ring as proof. "By the way, you do know you can buy all this stuff cheaper in China, right?" I clench my fist just enough for her to feel the lasso tighten again. "If what you say is true, why would Lee sic you on Catherine?"

"Are you jealous that he didn't send you instead?" She smiles. "How could he? I mean, despite being his loyal little lap dog, you have a propensity toward nobility. No matter how much you hated Catherine personally, he couldn't very well ask you to murder Evan's mother. Still, your visit gave me the perfect opportunity, so thanks for obliging." She winks at me. "Admit it—you're glad she's gone."

Catherine ruined my reputation in high school by starting a rumor that I'd lost my virginity with her boyfriend: Robert. She stole precious moments I could have had with my dying mother. Hell, she even stole my mother's apple pie recipe.

What doesn't kill us makes us stronger—and allows us to take vengeance on behalf of the innocent.

Would I have killed Catherine, even if the extermination had been government-sanctioned?

Yes, but only if she were threatening my family.

Instead, she gave me the greatest gift of all: her son, Evan.

I guess this is what Xia calls noble. But I'll be damned if I take Xia's word about Lee's opinion of me.

I'll give her the ultimate test, even if it is a lie. "You're right. My allegiance is to Lee, above anything else. That being said, I'll release you when you're in his custody, along with the evidence that you killed Catherine." I hold up the syringe.

Her eyes widen.

"And, by the way, I also have the intel that Catherine intended for me—so yes, you failed in your mission."

"You silly fool! If you think your president—"

Suddenly, we hit an air pocket deep enough that the plane drops a good ten feet. It's enough to shut anyone up, even a panicking hitwoman with nothing to lose.

Damn it, somewhere midair, I lose my grip on Xia. Maybe it's a good thing, because instinct tells me to put my hands up over my head to protect it.

However, Xia's instinct is to jerk the lasso off her neck with one hand while she shields her head from the ceiling with the other.

We both hit the floor on our knees, smacking it hard.

Before I can scramble onto my feet, she rolls far from my grasp and leaps up. In two seconds, she's by the bathroom vanity, where she grabs her toiletry bag—

Where she'd hidden a gun.

The next thing I know, she's got a Ruger SR22 pressed against my temple.

"Don't be stupid," I warn her. "If you shoot a gun in here, we'll lose cabin pressure, and we'll all die."

"My death sentence is assured either way. I don't mind taking you with me." She taps my temple with it. "Besides, at this close range, I won't miss."

"Neither will I." Jack is standing in the doorway. He has his Sig aimed at Xia.

"Ooooh, the boy toy plays rough," she coos. With her free hand, she jerks me closer so that I'm her human shield. "Go ahead, take your shot."

Don't mind if I do.

Ego is your enemy. Case in point: Xia's propensity to flirt, even when the object of her affection has a gun pointed in her direction, has given me the precious few seconds I need in order to flick off the needle cap on the syringe I hold in my pocket.

When I stab her hard in the jugular, she's still smiling at Jack through pursed lips.

But her simper is replaced by gasps as the Digitalis races through her. Still, she has enough energy to pull the trigger—

I hit her with an elbow to the gut before ducking out of the line of fire.

Jack is not so lucky.

The bullet pierces him in the head. Stunned, his hand goes to the wound: the right side of his head, just over his ear.

He reels backward into the galley as Xia hits the floor face down.

As I run to him, my scream fills the cabin.

I cradle his head in my lap and press my hand over the wound, ignoring the blood seeping through my fingers. Jack's eyes are fluttering and he's trying to speak, but no words come out. Still, his lips form the words *I love you* and *I'm sorry*.

Even if he could say them, I wouldn't be able to hear him, and not just because George is shouting over the intercom, "May Day! May Day! Request immediate emergency landing and an ambulance—" but because I am wailing so loudly and I can't hear anything over the beating of my heart.

———————————————————

17

Frost

———————————————————

The condensation and freezing of moisture in the air is known as frost. Tender plants will suffer extensive damage or die when exposed to it.

The same can happen to a relationship, seasoned or tender, if one of the partners can't forgive the other for an indiscretion.

Ask yourself: if he comes clean, can you forgive, let alone forget?

If not, put up a good front—at least until the frost has thawed.

(No, silly—not the one in your marriage! The one outside your window. When it does, it'll be easier to bury his body.)

JACK IS UNCONSCIOUS, BUT THE FACT THAT HE IS STILL BLEEDING

is a good thing. At least that is what I tell myself, especially when I consider the alternative.

All of this blood flowing out of him means his heart hasn't stopped. But when you hold the life of a loved one in your hands, seconds seem like hours, and minutes seem like days. Will we get him to the hospital in time?

The massive storm moving over the Midwest detoured our plane's flight path to the north and east. Apparently, God did us a favor, because at the moment the bullet entered Jack, we were only eight minutes away from Baltimore-Washington International Airport.

When we land, several cop cars and a fire truck are there to meet us, as is the ambulance that will whisk us the eleven miles to Johns Hopkins Hospital, where Ryan has arranged for Jack's emergency surgery to take place. The fireman and EMTs are real, but the cops are Acme cleaners--that is to say operatives adept at making ugly little problems like dead bodies and crime scenes go away without a trace.

In other words, no one will ever know what really happened to Xia.

The lifesaving ballet of the three emergency med techs fills me with awe. Noting that Jack is unconscious, one of the EMTs—his name tag says Jared— assesses the head wound: "Small entry wound above his right ear. No gray matter visible." He then applies the necessary pressure to staunch Jack's bleeding, while another medic—Jason— strips Jack of his clothes with trauma shears. The third medic, Kendra, assesses his head and body for other injuries, then makes sure nothing obstructs his airway.

before Jason and Jared lay him on a backboard and strap him down.

While Kendra gets behind the wheel, Jared and Jason heave him onto the gurney, which is then rolled down the airport's freestanding security ramp before he's loaded into the ambulance. I jump in back too. Before they can say anything, I pull out my Acme ID, showing I have the highest level of clearance. Jason raps Kendra's back window, and we're off.

JARED TAPS AN ARTERY IN JACK'S ARM IN ORDER TO INSERT A saline IV. Jason puts him on oxygen, then hooks him up to a heart monitor. I can hear Kendra calling the hospital's trauma team in order to alert it that a GSW trauma is en route.

The first eight minutes of the ride go quickly. Jared is on constant vigil: checking Jack's blood pressure, his pulse, and talking to him, to see if Jack will come to. At the same time, Jason has me filling in the blanks: about Jack's age, health issues, allergies, medical status, and how he ended up in the path of a bullet while in midair.

As you can imagine, his eyes widen when I say, "I'd tell you, but because your security clearance isn't high enough, I'd have to kill you."

That would be a much-needed moment of comic relief if the next thing out of Jared's mouth wasn't, "Patient crashing!"

The next thing I know, Jared is placing a bag-valve mask over Jack's mouth and nose to force oxygen into his lungs. He then positions himself over Jack and begins chest compressions, counting them off.

When this still doesn't get him breathing, Jason goes in with the hardware. I turn my head when he attaches the electrodes of the defibrillator and hold my breath as he shouts out, "Clear!" And I hear the telltale sound of the electric shock from the defibrillator jumping Jack's heart.

Finally, he yells, "Pulse!"

Jared and Jason slap high-fives.

Suddenly, the ambulance makes a turn so wide that the fluid bags are flung sideways on their poles. In anticipation of a quick stop, the EMTs brace themselves. Not me. I'm tossed forward and onto the floor. I look up to see Jack's fluid bags spinning on their hooks.

"Women drivers," Jason mutters. "Gotta love 'em."

How serene Jack looks, despite the chaos around him.

No, Jack, it is not your time to rest in peace.

Jack's saviors fling open the back doors and shove his gurney into the waiting arms of his receiving party—four ER personnel, male and female, nurses and doctors—who swirl around him like desperate dervishes, whose liturgy is made up of their patient's life support stats.

I run after them as they wheel him through the ER into a hallway leading to the surgery suites. I have to hold it together when Jason and Jared bar me from entering the OR, if only to ask, because I need someone to tell me something

—anything, even if it's not something I want to hear: "Will he survive?"

Their eyes meet over my head. "Miracles happen every day," Jason finally mutters, dubiously.

That's my cue to pray.

I guess this is one of those times where the least and most you can do are one and the same.

IT'S A FOUR-HOUR SURGERY. I'VE BEEN TOLD, "MAKE YOURSELF comfortable in the waiting room."

Talk about a poor choice of words. There is nothing comfortable about fear and anxiety and the interminable delay of knowledge. So, when I'm not praying, I'm pacing. And when I'm not pacing, I'm blaming myself for—

For what?

For falling in love with a man whose job always puts him in peril? Or for getting out of the line of fire instead of taking the bullet now embedded somewhere in his brain?

I collapse into a chair and bury my head in my hands. But I refuse to cry—at least, not until I know, one way or another.

I close my eyes and my mind to the inevitable: a life without Jack.

WHEN I FEEL A TAP ON MY SHOULDER, I PRACTICALLY LEAP OUT of my skin.

"Mrs. Stone?" I look up into a man's face, fatigued and scruffy, above green surgical scrubs. The name tag reads *Mario Martinez, MD.* "I just wanted to let you know that we've done all we can."

I collapse back into my chair. "So, Jack is…gone."

My partner. My love.

My life.

"No—"

It takes a minute for the word to winnow into my subconscious.

There is hope.

"—But it's still touch-and-go," Doctor Martinez warns me. "When we saw that there was no exit wound, we feared the worst. During the operation, resuscitation was needed, twice. Frankly, it's rare to operate when a patient has such a low Glasgow Coma Score." He winces. "Let me put it this way—it helps that he has friends in high places."

In other words, God. Well, and Ryan.

"The fact that the caliber of the bullet was small—a twenty-two—saved his life. It penetrated both the skin and the scalp, but luckily, not the skull."

I can't believe my ears. "That's good, right? But, all that blood loss—"

"One of the superficial external carotid arteries was nicked."

He holds up a .22 bullet. It is somewhat flattened, but

intact. "It was buried just beneath his scalp. His skull is fractured, but the bullet didn't penetrate it."

"Will he…survive?"

"We don't know yet. He's still in a coma. Even if he wakes up, the massive concussion he incurred may lead to a lifetime of tremors, or even brain damage. It's a waiting game."

"Doctor, may I go to him?"

He nods. "Follow me."

JACK IS MY SLEEPING PRINCE.

I force myself to block out the bandage wrapped around his head, and the fluid tubes and monitors attached to different parts of his lifeless body. Instead, I make myself remember his dry, cutting wit, and his boundless courage, and his deep, resonant voice, especially when he said, "I love you."

His eyes are closed, which is good, because I'd hate for him to see the tears flowing down my cheeks. I must keep it together. They say that it helps if you talk to coma patients. But since there's no manual listing other do's and don'ts, I have to wing it. I don't know whether or not it's okay for me to smother him with kisses, but that's what I do.

He can't comment back, so my non-stop chatter becomes a confessional. Whether Jack can hear me or not, I tell him how relieved I am that he's still alive, and that I feel guilty for having ducked without first checking to see if he was out of the line of fire, and that I'm sorry for all the times I should have listened to him but didn't.

I come clean with all the mistakes I know I've made in our relationship, no matter how big or small. More to the point, I promise that in the future I won't wait until he's in a coma to tell him when he's right.

And for that reason alone, he should wake up.

UNTIL DEATH DO US PART.

I wonder if I'll ever get to say those words to Jack.

In truth, the phrase does not conjure up fond memories. I shivered when I said it to Carl on our wedding day. The phrase, in French, was how Jack's wife, Valentina, chose to reach out to him after running off with Carl.

Now that both Carl and Valentina are dead, Jack and I were ready to move our lives forward, together.

Just thinking about it reminds me of Catherine's ring, deep in my pants pocket. I pull it out and stare down at it. Its large round-cut diamond is raised above the smaller stones, which are encrusted around the antique gold band. From its age, I presume it's a family heirloom.

For the first time, I notice that the diamond is a bit loose. It doesn't come off, but can be raised just enough to hold something within its prongs—

Something very thin—

A slim metal disk. It is a microdot.

Catherine's last words to me were *You've now got what you need.*

This must be what she meant.

She also said, *Remember—you promised.*

I was too late for her.

I hope this isn't the case for Jack too.

I reach for my phone and call Ryan.

"How is he doing?" Ryan's voice sounds anxious.

"They have him stabilized, but he's still in a coma. The bullet was found under his scalp—almost as flat as a pancake."

Ryan's attempt at a chuckle is weak. "He's lucky he's so hard-headed."

"I'll be honest with you—there's no telling how long he'll stay this way. When he wakes up—"

"You mean, *if* he wakes up." Ryan isn't expressing despair. As always, he's preparing for the worst-case scenario.

"No, Ryan! I mean what I say. *When* he awakens, they don't know what condition he'll be in." I try not to choke on my words. "There could be permanent brain damage. Or he could suffer tremors. In any regard, I'm staying by his side."

"Of course." He pauses, then adds, "I'm sure Aunt Phyllis and the children will feel the same way."

"One more thing, Ryan. Catherine gave Evan her wedding ring. She slipped a microdot under the setting. From what she hinted at, it may have concrete evidence to implicate President Chiffray as a member of the Quorum. And before Liang Xia died, the statements she made seem to add credence. She claimed that Lee sent her to exterminate Catherine for that very reason."

Ryan is silent for so long that I'm afraid the cell transmission somehow dropped out. Finally, he says, "Arnie is still waiting for the release of Catherine's body. I'll send him to Johns Hopkins first, to retrieve the ring."

I hang up.

I'd love to crawl into bed beside Jack. Instead, I move one of the room's two guest chairs as close to him as I can, and I inch my hand under his patient gown so that I can place it on his chest, directly over his heart. That way, I can feel it beating, if just barely.

"Yes, I'll marry you," I whisper, as if this is the magical phrase that will rouse him from his fateful slumber.

But it doesn't.

I PACE THE FLOOR UNTIL ARNIE SHOWS UP TO COURIER THE microdot back to Acme.

"You'll call as soon as you crack it, right?" I ask him.

Arnie nods, but he can't pull his eyes away from Jack. Who can blame him? The beeping monitors are bad enough. Add to that the bandage covering Jack's head, his gray pallor and bloodless lips, I'd been struck speechless too.

I don't have to tell him to pray for our dear friend. I watch as he crosses himself.

Before turning to leave, he kisses me on my forehead.

I hate seeing the pity in his eyes.

18

Heeling In

When you don't have time to give a plant the right home, you can provide a temporary one for it by setting it into a shallow trench and covering its roots with soil so that it has the protection it needs until it is ready to be permanently planted. Gardeners call this process "heeling in."

Obviously, this is different from teaching a dog to heel, which, teaches him to move with you, by staying next to your right leg. Usually, this involves weeks of training with a leash and some treats.

Heeling in a human is somewhat more complicated. A leash puts you on the right course. A whip may be needed to show him who's boss. However, if the human can't be trained, the shallow trench will once again be put to good use.

Only this time, what you plant there will find a permanent home.

THE NURSE SHAKES ME GENTLY. "MRS. STONE—"

I sit up with a start. *Oh, my God, did Jack die while I was sleeping?*

But no, the monitor's slow, constant beep hasn't changed.

It's been two days since Jack was shot. The nurses are kind about my constant vigil. They've learned to move around me, as if I'm just another piece of furniture.

This one notices my hand over Jack's heart, and shifts her eyes so that I can't see the sadness within them. She is no stranger to grief. If he doesn't wake soon from his coma, they'll try to convince me to let him slip away naturally.

I can't. Not yet, anyway.

Before she turns back, she forces a smile. "I'm sorry to have startled you. I didn't mean to wake you because of any change in Mr. Craig's condition, but because he has a special guest."

I glance around the room. The fatigue that mists my brain fades instantly when I see whom she means:

Lee Chiffray.

A broad-shouldered man in a black suit stands in front of the transom beside the room's closed door. He is part of the president's Secret Service detail.

Lee doesn't follow my gaze. He's too busy living up to the nurse's impression of a compassionate statesman. "Thank you, nurse," he says, all the while patting her hand as he walks her to the threshold.

She practically floats out the door. I doubt she'll wash her hand for at least a week. Perhaps I should request a different nurse to change Jack's bandage.

Lee walks over to the bed. He purses his lips at the scenario in front of him: Jack's head in bandages, and the lethargic monitor reading. Finally, he murmurs, "I'm sorry he got shot, Donna."

"Kind of you to say." I can't keep the frost out of my voice. If what Xia and Catherine said is true, he is the reason Jack is now hovering between life and death.

Oops, the nurse left her surgical cart behind. I pocket a scalpel. You never know when it'll come in handy.

"I talked to his attending physician," Lee says. "He assures me they're doing all they can to save him."

I shrug. "How did you hear about Jack?"

"Ryan called me."

"Oh? What else did he tell you?"

"Beyond the fact that Catherine was killed too? He also divulged that you were in the process of apprehending her assassin when Jack was shot."

"And I presume you know the assassin was Liang Xia." I wait for his flinch.

Instead, recognition comes with a frown. "Isn't that the same MSS operative who was involved in China's attempts to poison our crops?"

"It wasn't China, Lee. It was the Quorum. And, by the way, Secretary of Agriculture Harkness knew of a threat, and chose to do nothing about it. As a reward for keeping his mouth shut, I'm sure there's some fat bank account with his name on it."

Lee's eyes harden. "If that's true, I'll have him arrested immediately."

I take a step closer. "But, you already knew about his role in this, didn't you?"

"What? How would I?" He stares down at me, perplexed. "Donna, what is this about? Are you saying that I'd poison my own country?"

"Yes. You'd have a lot to gain from it: power and money, let alone keeping the world in a state of fear and terror." I take a step closer. "Before she died, Xia claimed it was you who sent her to assassinate Catherine."

"That's ridiculous! I'd already made my deal with Catherine. She was to get a full pardon on my last day in office. You knew this."

"Yes, that may have been the original plan—until Catherine attempted to change your little bargain." I watch his eyes narrow in anger at my accusation. "Lee, Catherine got in touch with me because she had evidence that you are the head of the Quorum."

My remark stuns him into silence. When he finally finds his tongue, it's to growl, "She was making a crazy accusation. She couldn't have anything of the sort, because it doesn't exist!" He looks me in the eye. "Donna, you of all people shouldn't have believed her."

"How about Xia? She swore that the kill order on Catherine came from you."

"I don't give orders to MSS operatives, Mrs. Stone. For God's sake, I'm the President of the United States—or have you forgotten?" His anger makes him stupid. He grabs my left arm and pulls me close to him. His eyes search mine for the hope that I believe him.

I murmur, "How could I ever forget?"

"Since they're both dead, you'll have to take my word, Donna," he mutters.

Good for Ryan. He didn't tell Lee about Catherine's microdot.

Our bodies are mere inches apart. Lee's eyes drop to my lips.

If they'd dropped as low as my wrist, he'd see I'm clenching the scalpel and I'm ready to use it.

But I don't. Not because I don't reciprocate the longing in his eyes, but because Jack's heart monitor seems to be revving up, like a Harley climbing out of a mud hole.

Lee and I look over at Jack in time to see his eyes blink open. His torso rises slightly from the bed. He croaks, "Donna…"

I toss off Lee's arm in order to run to Jack's side and smother him with kisses.

"I guess this means you've reconsidered my proposal," Jack murmurs.

"No, I was hoping you'd consider mine." I sit down on the bed facing him, and I take his hand. Holding it tight, I declare, "Jack Craig, my love, my soul mate—I can't fathom my world without you. Will you marry me?"

"Hell yeah, baby. I thought you'd never ask."

He couples his answer with a tender kiss.

When I turn around, Lee is gone.

Jack shifts slowly so that he can see too. "Was that—?"

"Um…yeah—Lee."

He shakes his head. "Figures. For a moment there, I'd mistaken him for the Grim Reaper."

"That may not be too far from the truth."

From the look on Jack's face, he's curious as to what I mean by that, but the full story will have to wait. Now that POTUS and his security posse are clearing the building, the nurses and doctors flood into the room to revel in that little miracle called life.

It's okay. Jack and I will have the rest of our lives to catch up on everything he missed.

Tendril Loving Care

Tendrils are twisting and clinging growth on vines that allow plants to attach themselves to a trellis for support.

Humans also grow, and in the process, sometimes they cling.

It's an honor to provide support to someone you love. If they prove worthy of your care, adoration, and devotion, by all means hold on for dear life. You'll both thrive.

GEORGE IS WAITING AT BWI TO TAKE US HOME. ACME'S IN-house medicine man, Doctor Fleishman, has accompanied him.

"Because we'll be flying at a high enough altitude, Ryan felt we should play it safe," he assures us. "I'll use the flight time to observe Jack, test his memory and motor skills, and clue you in on some things you can do to keep him comfortable at home."

Jack grins at me. I presume he had his own idea of what we could be doing with this time to ourselves, considering all the wonderful play spaces on this plane. Oh well, his Mile-High club fantasy will just have to wait.

We've just reached cruising altitude when Ryan's call comes through. I put it on speaker.

Ryan's voice booms through the cabin. "Arnie hacked Catherine's microdot."

"Don't keep us in suspense," Jack chides him.

"Frankly, I think we should wait until we're together, and not just because it's truly too sensitive for airwaves. Frankly, I can't wait to see the look on your face when you see Catherine's intel."

"Well, that's just peachy-keen," I mutter. "It'll be gnawing at me for the next five hours! What am I supposed to do, twiddle my thumbs?"

Ryan laughs. "Take a nice hot shower."

"Hardee-har-har." So much for getting the last laugh.

I'll admit it: I could certainly use one, and the bathroom shows no sign of the struggle that took place just a few days ago. Jack's blood has been wiped clean, the marble floors and counters sparkle, and the smell of rosemary wafts through the cabin.

It's not as if I expect Xia's ghost to rise from the steam created by the state-of-the-art Thunderhead rain showerhead, but I think I'll pass anyway.

The memory of Jack's near-fatal assault will stay with me

for quite some time. The scar above his ear is reminder enough of how close I came to losing him.

JACK WINCES AS I BOB AND WEAVE THROUGH SIX LANES OF I-405 in the i8. "Don't worry," I assure him. "I have things under control."

"Great, because I've spent too much time in a coma already."

"Oh, ye of little faith!" I shout over the *basso profundo* blasts from the two eighteen-wheelers, apparently miffed at my dexterity in squeezing between them.

As exhilarating as it is to have him alive again and at my side, maybe he's right about slowing down.

At least, until we get hitched. I don't plan on dragging a corpse down the aisle.

RYAN FROWNS WHEN I DECLARE, "GIVE, QUEENIE."

Dominic winces, whereas Jack, Abu, Emma, and Arnie duck their heads, as opposed to showing their smirks. Okay, yeah, I'm the only one who gets away with talking smack to Ryan.

That's okay. He always has a way of making me pay for the privilege.

He coughs before going into the spiel Jack and I have been waiting for, these past six hours. "Catherine had the goods on the Quorum alright," Ryan confirms, "thanks to her husband, Robert. He questioned the actual monetary sources coming from her biggest Super PAC, and tried to get her to refuse its funds. To prove his point, he hired an international team of investigators to track down the source of every dollar donated. But, instead of it scaring her straight, Catherine held onto it, in the hope of using it as a trump card. You'll see why in a minute."

He taps Arnie on the shoulder.

A photo appears on the conference room wall screen. It's an organizational chart. Twelve companies fan out in a circle like spokes in a wheel. "Each of these international conglomerates has its tentacles in banking, agribusiness, petrochem, biotech, defense contracting, software development, cloud security, media, transportation, or a combination of three or more of these industries."

"Graffias International is on the list," Jack points out.

Arnie nods. "Yep, but unfortunately, because it's a privately held company based in Switzerland, Acme's corporate intel division drew blanks on its leadership personnel, which are masked to all outside sources."

"Apparently, Robert's investigators had better luck," Ryan declares. "They hacked into the company's secure cloud and came up with three corporate officers. The CEO is this man."

A photo appears on the screen: It shows a handsome executive in his mid-forties: dark skin, deep-set eyes, high cheekbones. "His name is Salem Rahmin al-Sadah. His family made its billions as one of the investment advisors to the Saudi's Prince Faisal."

That's got my attention. "Great work if you can get it."

"It's certainly paid off for him," Ryan agrees, "and for the chairman of the board for Graffias too."

His picture fades into another: that of Eric Weber, the German operative who was one of the Quorum's original members. In fact, it was Eric who recruited Carl as a double agent. But when Carl decided to reinvent the Quorum after his own image, he targeted Eric for extermination.

Needless to say, Eric took the hint and disappeared off the face of the earth.

After Carl blackmailed Lee into appointing him as our country's Director of Intelligence, Jack and I found Eric's hideout: a French wine country chateau. We thought we had convinced him that he should testify about Carl's many acts of treason. Instead, Eric disappeared again.

Now we know where he ended up—back where he started, as one of the leaders of the Quorum.

"Well, what do you know?" I murmur.

"Trust me," Ryan warns, "it gets even better."

Eric's face is replaced by a woman's: that of the First Lady, Babette Breck Chiffray.

Jack whistles softly. "So, what's your guess, Ryan? Is she fronting for Lee?"

"Even so, aren't her assets and income also put in a blind trust while he's in office?" I counter. "Or does Lee even know about her ownership of this company? If it wasn't part of Breck International's holdings when his company—Global

World Industries—purchased it, he may be unaware of her involvement with it."

Jack's eyes narrow. "Thanks to Catherine, the proof is right here in front of us, as to who runs the Quorum. And if what Xia said is true, that she took her kill order from Lee, he knows alright."

I shake my head. "Catherine was coy about the meaning of this intel. Her exact words about Lee were, 'I'd like to be there to see the look on his face when you confront him.' For all we know, she was talking about breaking the news about Babette."

"It's possible," Ryan concedes.

"And when I questioned Lee at the hospital, he was downright angry because I accused him of being Quorum," I add. "He also denied contacting Xia, whom he referred to as MSS, which indicates he may not have known she's now a Quorum operative."

"He may be telling the truth," Arnie declares.

Jack and I turn to stare at him. "Say that again?" we say in unison.

"I hacked Xia's cell phone," he explains. "Yes, she did get some texts—not calls—from the White House. One is feeling her out for the hit on Catherine. Another agrees to her terms, and a third received validation of the hit, and provided evidence of the payoff. But that doesn't necessarily mean they were sent from POTUS. Even descrambled, the only ID from the texting source is a number: 362433."

Interesting. "Xia also claimed that there was some...well,

I guess you'd call it sexting between her and the White House."

Arnie blushes. "It's true, there were a couple of spicy ones. Okay, yeah, vulgar, really. The last one had the deets of a liaison in Georgetown that was supposed to take place on Xia's next trip stateside, which would have been in a couple of weeks."

"If it's a private residence, let's find out who owns it," Ryan orders Arnie. "If it's a hotel, get intel on who made the reservation. We've got to follow the crumbs."

"Sure, let's stake it out," Jack suggests. "If it isn't Lee, her liaison will turn up. But if it's him…"

Of course, he thinks the contact will be a no-show because he presumes that it's Lee.

"And if no one shows, we have to follow up with the leads we have," Ryan says, "any way we can."

He means reconnaissance on the Chiffrays—both of them.

Oh, boy, *that* should be fun.

Jack laughs. "I guess that means Lee and Babette are on the guest list for the wedding."

"*What?*" Everyone turns to stare at him—then at me.

"Yep, it's official," I declare. "I proposed, and Jack accepted."

"How perfectly splendid, old chap!" Dominic slaps him on the back. "I insist on throwing your bachelor party."

"Spiffy!" I respond oh so sweetly. But to Jack I mutter, "Don't hold your breath, dear. Acts of nature, you know. By the way, should there be a fire at Chateau Fleming prior to the event, do you think he'll call it off?"

"You wouldn't dare," Jack warns me. "Donna…Donna? Answer me."

Before I have a chance to either confirm or deny, Ryan says, "Since you brought up the guest list, as far as the Chiffrays are concerned—"

"Yeah, yeah whatever. We'll take it under advisement!" I exclaim, as I grab Jack's hand, and jerk him out the door with me.

There will be no more discussion about the wedding until we talk to my children about something even more important: my marriage to Jack, and what it means for them.

"CAN WE SEE THE HOLE?" IT'S THE FIRST QUESTION JEFF ASKS Jack after locking him in a five-minute hug.

Trisha shakes her head adamantly. "Ewwww, yuck! *NO!*"

By the way Mary and Evan exchange nods, I guess I know how they'd vote on the topic.

"Don't be such a scaredy-cat," Aunt Phyllis admonishes my youngest. On the other hand, Jack gets a nudge. "Go ahead, Braveheart, show us the big bad booboo that had us gnawing our fingers to the bone."

Jack laughs. "Okay, but remember, you asked for it."

He lifts the bandage slowly.

Everyone leans forward, fascinated.

"Omigod!" Mary whispers softly. Her smile fades as

morbid curiosity turns to cold dread. She drapes her arm around Jack's neck. "I'm sorry, Jack."

Jack shrugs. "That's what happens when you don't duck."

"I hate guns," Trisha declares.

"Frankly, I do too—when they're used by bad people," Jack admits.

"How long will it take for you to heal?" Evan asks.

"The doc says I should stay off my feet as much as possible, at least for the next six weeks, and to forego any strenuous exertion. So everyone else has to pick up the slack and help your mom."

The kids nod.

"In fact, your mom and I will need your help with something else." Jack smiles up at me.

I take his hand in mine. "Jack and I are getting married."

"About damn time," Jeff mutters.

He gets cuffed in the ears for that—by Jack on one side, and me on the other.

"And the way we see it, it's a family affair," I continue. I turn to Aunt Phyllis. "I'm hoping you'll give me away."

She snorts. "I've been trying to do that for years!"

Jack is laughing so hard that he's choking.

I smack his arm, then turn to my son. "Jeff, will you walk me down the aisle?" I ask.

"Sure, Mom." He honors me with a thumbs-up.

"Mary, will you be my maid of honor?"

She answers me with a kiss.

Jack holds out his hand for Evan to shake. "Are you up for being a groomsman?"

Evan takes it. "Only if I can also plan the bachelor party."

Mary and I both give him the evil eye.

"Dominic offered too," I say slyly. "Perhaps the two of you can coordinate."

Evan snorts. "What, are you kidding? I'm not talking finger sandwiches and tea cozies here!"

At this point, the last thing he needs to know is Dominic's perennial Number One ranking for "Undercover Lover," the poll run by the female spooks and covert operatives all over the world.

All in good time, dearie. All in good time.

"Can I get a new flower girl dress?" Trisha begs. She adds solemnly, "I'm sure Arnie and Emma told me I could never wear the one I wore for them to anyone else's wedding —*ever.*"

Trisha's fib sets everyone laughing again.

I chuck her under the chin. "I don't think you're right about that. But, yes, all of the Stone women are getting new dresses."

Mary's smile fades. "I guess we won't be the Family Stone anymore."

Jack shakes his head. "You know, I'd be honored if each and every one of you took my name. But it's a decision that is yours alone to make. As far as I'm concerned, what you call yourself doesn't matter—only that, together, we call ourselves 'family'."

Emotions shift through my children like a rising sun on a

stained glass window. For a moment, their faces are dark-
ened by their fears of what this change might truly mean in
their lives.

What part of their identities will they be giving up?

But then, very slowly, their eyes light up with the realization that Jack is, and has always been, what they've always
wanted:

The loving father who makes their mother happy.

Mary thinks for a moment. "Hmmm, *'Mary Craig.'* I like
the ring of that."

Mrs. Donna Craig...

Yep, it works.

It's going to be one hell of a wedding.

—THE END—

Research for This Book

When plotting my novels, I ask myself the question, "Can this happen? Is it plausible?"

Even the plotting of a light mystery starts with copious research, especially when it includes such topics as bioterrorism, biogenetics, and an industry as complex as agriculture. In my case, advance research for *The Housewife Assassin's Garden of Deadly Delights* began with conversations with professionals in particular fields, as well as articles in professional journals and established newspapers.

Here are some interesting facts that are stranger than fiction:

1. Can plants carry a virus harmful to humans?

Yes. Ebola is a perfect example. Fatalities from this filovirus can run anywhere from fifty to ninety percent. Deaths can happen within a week of exposure. The Marburg, Lassa and Machupo viruses can be harmful, and in some cases fatal. As of the time I write this, there are no vaccines for these viruses.

2. Can a virus cause cancer?

Yes. In the course of researching plot points for this novel, I stumbled upon a plant virus known as cytomegalovirus, or CMV, which causes a particularly aggressive form of brain cancer in humans in conjunction with the patients' genetic markers. CMV is quick acting, and deadly. Whereas there is no vaccine as of yet, the Brain Tumor Society and the NIH are funding a study at Duke University in the hope of developing one.

3. Will swine eat humans?

Yes, there is a precedent. Recent incidents include a case in which an Italian mobster boasted of a rival's death-by-swine on a phone call intercepted by local police. Another sad incident was that of a seventy-year-old Oregon farmer whose only remains were his dentures. Another incident took place in Romania, where a farmer's wife was knocked unconscious and was being devoured when her husband found her and pulled her out of the pig pen. She died in the hospital.

4. As for whether cows attack humans...

A six-year four-state study proves it sometimes

happens. In my scenario, I had the consumption of corn tainted with a virus that leads to brain cancer as further motivation.

5. Can a person get killed by getting tossed under a corn harvester?

In December 2014, a Canadian farmer was a recent fatality. The article I found in the incident also notes that he was the third such fatality—that is, via farm equipment—in the local area.

Again, I look for plausibility. This is, after all, a work of fiction.

You can find the articles referred to here on my website:

www.authorprovocateur.com/research-notes-for-garden-of-deadly-delights.html

How to Reach Josie

To write Josie, go to:
mailfromjosie@gmail.com

To find out more about Josie, or to get on her eLetter list for
book launch announcements, go to her website:
www.JosieBrown.com

You can also find her at:

www.AuthorProvocateur.com

twitter.com / JosieBrownCA

facebook.com / josiebrownauthor

pinterest.com / josiebrownca

instagram.com / josiebrownnovels